SAVING HER

SAVING HER

A Novel

CHRISTIAN MCPHERSON

| N₁ | O₂ | N₁

CANADA

Library and Archives Canada Cataloguing in Publication

McPherson, Christian, author
Saving her / Christian McPherson.

ISBN 978–1–926942–95–7 (paperback)

I. Title.

PS8625.P53S28 2015   C813'.6   C2015–904982–2

Printed and bound in Canada on 100% recycled paper.

Now Or Never Publishing
#313, 1255 Seymour Street
Vancouver, British Columbia
Canada V6B 0H1

nonpublishing.com
Fighting Words.

We gratefully acknowledge the support of the Canada Council for the Arts
and the British Columbia Arts Council for our publishing program.

for Shelley Little
thanks for introducing me to my wife

"Cross my heart and hope to die,
stick a needle in my eye."
~ Children's Oath

PROLOGUE

Julie had always been a natural athlete, a natural competitor. As a child she never wanted to walk anywhere, she always ran. She would say, "Race you there," and take off running. At school she would play on the monkey bars until her hands were blistered and bleeding. Swimming was no exception, always full tilt.

It happened at their cottage the summer she was eight. Her brother had just turned ten. The neighbours three cottages down had put in a new floating dock twenty metres off their property. Julie had said to her brother Luke, "Race you around it?" Luke was more bookish, but by no means overweight or lazy. He didn't see the point in sports. Found all of them rather silly. But he liked competing with his sister. He had put his hand over his eyes and squinted as he looked out upon the lake.

"Okay, you're on," he had said, putting down his adventure novel. He took off running towards the water where his sister waited.

When they rounded the dock in the water, Julie had taken the lead by almost a metre. Sometimes, as she suspected, Luke would let her win. Not this time though. He seemed to be struggling to keep up with her. She was fast. Like an otter, her swimming instructor would say. She didn't look back, she was going for it, pouring everything she had into it. When she reached the shoreline at the point where she could stand up, she did. Her father was standing on the shore holding a beer. He was smiling.

"I won!" Julie announced, spinning around to face Luke. The water was calm and smooth, the inky reflection of the cedar trees bleeding out from the shoreline.

She spun back to her father.

"Where's your brother?" he asked putting down his beer.

"He was behind me," she said.

"Where is your brother!" he yelled, now running towards her.

"I don't know," she said and began to cry.

"LUKE!" her father shouted. That's when she saw the look on his face. It was the look of her father's world coming apart and it burned into her memory.

"Get your mother, call for help!" he screamed. She did, and afterwards watched as her father dove down into the water, over and over, each time coming up screaming her brother's name, always coming up without him. She watched as Mr. Jamison came roaring across the lake in his fishing boat. The neighbours were all standing on their docks, hands over their eyes, watching. Another neighbour, Ray, dove into the water with a pair of goggles and swam toward the floating dock.

It would be almost three hours before the police divers pulled up her brother's body.

★

Luke's room sat unchanged for almost two years. It was a museum, a place where one would go to look at things from the past, to remember how things had been before. Julie caught her father several times sitting on Luke's bed with a drink clutched in his hand, bottle on the floor ready for a refill. Her parents kept his door shut most of the time. She often wondered what her father thought about when he sat in there. Did he imagine what they would be doing together? Playing catch? Playing road hockey? Teaching him how to drive the car? One day her father caught her looking at the rocks Luke had collected and kept on his shelf. There was a smooth speckled rock which resembled vermiculite. Luke had picked it up on the beach during their Christmas vacation in Cuba. She was rubbing the rock against her cheek when her father appeared in the doorway.

"Put it back," he said.

"I loved him too. He was my brother, you know. You're not the only one who gets to be sad. And besides," she said, "you never loved him when he was alive, only now that he's dead."

He stepped into the room and slapped her across the face. Her mother followed him into the room.

"I'm sorry . . ." he said, holding his hand against his chest as if it were a loaded gun which had gone off by itself.

"Jesus Christ, Bob," her mother said. Julie put down the rock, stepped around her father and stood by her mother. Julie said with her back still to her father, "I loved him too." Her mother, who smelled of lavender, hugged her. She cried. They all cried.

The next day, Julie walked by her brother's room to find her mother packing all his stuff into cardboard boxes.

"Do you want anything?" she asked, glancing up.

"Just the rock," Julie answered, striding into the room and scooping it up.

★

After that, her father was never the same. A part of him had been taken away. He seemed to struggle with everything. He was defeated by brushing his teeth, tying his shoes. Eating became a mountain he couldn't climb. His clothing became loose fitting. His face turned hollow and sullen. Even at Christmas his mood never rose beyond a tepid pleasure. He drank heavily at times.

Her parents sold the cottage the following year. It was shortly afterwards that Julie awoke in the middle of the night to find her father sitting on the edge of her bed. She could smell the liquor on his breath.

"Daddy?" she said, sitting up.

At first he didn't say anything, remaining still, staring at the floor.

"Daddy, what is it, what's wrong?" she asked.

"I want you to know," he paused as if he was choosing his words very carefully, "I want you to know that it's not your fault. It wasn't your fault, what happened to your brother."

Julie said nothing. She did blame herself. She never said it though, to her mother or to her father. It had been eating her up, giving her nightmares.

"Julie, do you understand it's not your fault?" her father slurred.

"I shouldn't have asked him to race me," she said.

"Listen to me," he said, placing his hand on her leg. "It's not your fault. I want you to race. I want you to start swimming again. I talked to your coach."

"I don't want to."

"I want you to. I need you to. You need to do it for your brother, because he can't."

Julie remained quiet. Her father stood up and stopped in the doorway, his back to her. "I just wanted to tell you that," he said and walked away.

After that little 'talk,' Julie took it upon herself to do what her father had asked. She got back into swimming and entered competitions. She did it for herself, but she also for Luke and for her father in hopes of making him happy once more. However, as her trophies and medals piled up in her room, her father's despondent condition grew worse. His drinking became more frequent and more severe. He would take her to swim meets, cheer from the stands, take her out for a soda afterwards and tell her with a slur what a great job she had done, how proud of her he was. But it never felt quite right. His love never seemed 100 percent genuine. It felt, for lack of a better word, forced. Maybe he resented her, blamed her? Did he lie to her? She didn't think so. Before Luke died, Julie suspected her father actually favoured her because she was so athletic. She was the boy he always wanted. He had treated Luke at times like he was a disappointment. Luke didn't enjoy playing catch or throwing a Frisbee around; he would rather read or play with his Lego. Julie was always up for it. Her dad was similar to her, athletic, outdoorsy. But when Luke died, something died inside her father too. When she couldn't bring it back by winning medal after medal, Julie did what she always did, she tried even harder. She spent the rest of her childhood trying to be two kids. She did the things she loved to do: swimming, biking, and fishing. But then she would also do the things Luke used to love to do: reading, building castles, and drawing.

The day after Julie turned 16, her father drank himself to death.

PART I
RUNNING

I

It always ended horribly. It always began the same way. It began with stale smells of plastic and jet fuel, smells you'd normally encounter making the journey down the narrow aisle of any jumbo airliner towards your seat. Her boarding pass clutched in one hand, her shoulder bag awkwardly slung over her belly as if it were her expected child, Julie kept looking at the seat numbers printed below the luggage bins. She was checking them against her ticket, as if somehow the number might have changed, or possibly she'd read it wrong the first eight times. 21B. When she found her seat, she stowed her bag, sat down and quickly fastened her seatbelt—a kind of psychological Band-Aid against her fear of flying. She leaned back hard, pressing her cranium into the headrest, closing her eyes and rocking her head side to side while listening to the muted hissing of the overhead air nozzles. Exhaling, she sat forward opening her eyes, trying her best to relax. An overweight man with crimson cheeks and notable perspiration was struggling with his carry-on bag. He was pushing at it, pounding it with his fist as if he were in a fight. The passengers coming down the aisle had come to a standstill waiting for the battle to finish. Eventually an airline attendant came shimmying up through the traffic jam. Wiping his brow, the man took his seat while the attendant took over. Clearly the bag was too big. The attendant told the man as much, and to the relief of the other impatient passengers took the bag away to stow it at the front of the plane, freeing up the aisle.

A little girl with bright blonde hair pulled her mother's hand, dragging her to the seats across from Julie.

"We're here! We're here!" the little girl exclaimed. "Can I have the window seat, mom?"

"Yes, yes," answered her mother, barely able to keep up. "Somebody's excited," she said to Julie.

"I can see that," said Julie smiling, wishing she shared the young girl's enthusiasm for flying.

"We're going to see my dad!" said the child, peering around her mother's waist as she stowed their jackets.

"Oh, where does he live?" asked Julie.

"Where we're going, silly," stated the child.

And this puzzled Julie. Where were they all going? Why didn't she know that? Then she saw the girl's T-shirt. Written in a kind of Seventies psychedelic bubbled scrawl were the words SAN FRANCISCO. Of course, how could she forget that?

The plane filled up as everyone took their seats. The little screen embedded in the headrest before her initiated the pre-flight safety video, zen-like attendants performing smooth demonstrations of life vests, oxygen masks and emergency exits. Julie watched with a detached puzzlement. Why did it seem so . . . familiar? Was it déjà vu?

When the door of the plane closed, an overwhelming sense of doom washed over Julie, the kind of sensation she got when the safety bar was clamped down over her knees on a rollercoaster. This was it. She was now locked into this stomach-churning ride for the duration.

Thankfully, the seat beside her remained empty as the plane began to roll backwards and away from the gate. She watched the little girl peer out the window. then turn to her mother and announce excitedly that they were moving. The mother shot Julie a smile which she dutifully reciprocated, trying to disguise the fear she felt.

As the plane taxied down the runway, bobbing and swaying gently as it went, Julie felt a sweat break out down her back. She gripped the armrests and looked out the little oval window at the grass and asphalt floating by. A windsock fluttered lazily as the plane turned and came to a stop. This was it. When the tower said it was time to go, they would go. Julie hated take-offs. *Hated* them. She knew it was irrational. She understood the physics behind it. But no matter how much she thought about it, she couldn't quite wrap her mind around the notion of this enormous tin can flying through the air. And with all that explosive jet fuel too.

The whine from the engines preceded the acceleration. The plane was moving. Fast. Julie felt herself being sucked back against the seat, as if her soul were being torn from her body. She hated this sensation. It was as if she were connected to the plane, plugged into it. Spine to nerve, nerve to seat, seat to wheels, and when they lifted off the ground she had the sensation she might be sick.

The plane ascended at a sharp angle, then pitched hard to the left. Julie could see the streets, the cars, and all the little blue circles and squares of swimming pools in the backyards of all those little houses, whizzing by her window. Toy houses. And there again was that feeling, that feeling something wasn't right. Like walking into a room and forgetting what it was she was there to do. She couldn't put her finger on it. What was it?

The plane leveled out and continued its gradual climb. Julie squirmed in her seat and took some long deep breaths, trying as best she could to calm down. She looked over at the mother and little girl. "Look, mom, I can see our building," said the girl and that's when it happened.

A large bright flash of light. White light. And noise so loud that Julie was temporarily deafened. A high note held on a synthesizer rang in her head. Black smoke and debris filled the cabin. Air masks sprung down like medical marionettes as the plane spun right and began to plummet. Julie gripped the armrests. The ringing in her ears disappeared into the screams of passengers. Flames shot out of the smoke from the front section of the plane and danced against the top of the fuselage. She fumbled for her mask as the pilot struggled to level out the plane. The engines oscillated in speed as the plane pitched back and forth. A flight attendant came ping-ponging up the aisle from the rear swaddling a fire extinguisher. She held out the red canister and squeezed the nozzle. The plane jerked violently. She lost her balance, smacking her head against the luggage bins, and sprawled backwards. She let go of the extinguisher and it rolled back down the aisle. Julie tried to reach for it but missed. The mother across the aisle was yelling for help. The seats in front of them were on fire. Julie saw the terror on their faces. She had only seen that look, that level of terror, once before. She understood. This was the woman's child. You would do anything to protect your child. Now here they were and there was nothing that could be done. Julie fought with her belt buckle but it wouldn't come free. She was panicking. She knew she needed to calm down and focus if she was going to help. The plane dipped and the fire extinguisher came rolling back towards her seat. This time she was able to grab it. She lifted it and aimed the nozzle at the flaming seats across the aisle. She pushed against the silver handle and nothing happened. The mother screamed. Julie saw the flames had leapt onto the child's sleeve and the mother's pants. The little girl cried hysterically. Julie clawed again at her seatbelt. Nothing. She couldn't get the thing off. She tried pushing on the handle of the extinguisher once more. Nothing.

"Help us!" screamed the mother.

"I'm trying," said Julie.

"HELP US!"

Julie kept trying, kept pushing the lever. Nothing came out. The little girl screamed. Then the mother did too.

"SAVE HER!"

Julie jolted awake. She was disoriented and didn't understand the layout of the room. The sheets were wet, soaked in sweat. Ryan lay next to her, his back to her. He stirred, but didn't roll over.

"Did you have it *again?*" he asked without moving.

"Yes," she said.

It always ended horribly. Always with that mother yelling, "Save her." But Julie always awoke before she could. This was not a good way to start a race, especially not this one, her first Ironman. She already felt exhausted.

The hotel clock displayed 4:45. Fifteen minutes before the alarm was to go off. Race time was 7:00AM. She got up to take a shower even though she was about to swim 3.8 kilometres in

Okanagan Lake. Julie never felt truly awake until she had her shower, never felt ready for the day. It helped her clear her head. When she closed her eyes, she could still see the little girl on fire, screaming. She made the water warmer and closed her eyes, letting it spray against her face and head. She breathed through her mouth, letting the water fall from her lips and nose while she focused on visualising the first leg of the race: running into the water, finding a good position, and swimming around the huge orange buoys. She imagined herself from a short distance, as if she were the cameraman on a reality show following her every move. Then she played out the second section in her head: exiting the water, changing in the transition area, stepping astride her bike and pedalling 180 kilometers. Finally she visualized the final section: racking her bike, changing and heading out onto the run. A full marathon—42.2 KM. She saw herself crossing the finish line, fists held high in the air. Then she flashed to the little girl on fire.

It was exactly three years ago to the day that the dream first occurred. It started when Julie began to train seriously for the Ironman. The first time she had it, she didn't think anything of it. Chalked it up to stress. After it happened the second time, she cut down on her coffee. It became a monthly event. When it occurred, it often left her so shaken that she had to call in sick for work. She thought it might be connected to her period, a latent desire to have children, to protect them. Then the dream began to happen more regularly. She incorporated yoga and meditation into her exercise regime and this seemed to help. The dream's frequency slowed. Last year she only had it every second month, then only every four. It had been almost six months since she'd last had it. She thought she was done with it. Last night was a setback. And on this big day, the day she had been working toward for so long.

She turned off the shower and pulled back the curtain. Ryan was at the sink, brushing his teeth.

"You okay?"

"Yeah, I'm good," she said. She wasn't sure she was, but then again she wasn't sure she wasn't. She didn't want Ryan's pity, a possible motivational pep talk. She knew she had done her home-work. It was that fucking dream. Why today of all days?

"Are you going to shower?" she asked.

"No, I'll go down ahead and grab you some breakfast. I'll come back and shower when you're on the bike," he said.

Ryan was good like that. Sweet natured. She slapped him on the ass on her way out of the bathroom. The TV was on the Weather Channel. Sunny day, clouding over in the afternoon with a 30% chance of rain. High of 25. Perfect, she thought.

"Looks good," he said, emerging from the bathroom.

"Fantastic."

"You want the usual?" he asked, opening the hotel door.

"Banana, toast, and a hardboiled egg," she said, drying her hair with a towel while checking over her racing gear.

"Right. See you down there," he said and disappeared, the door clicking shut behind him.

She threw on her bathing suit and shorts, then a T-shirt over top. She faced the mirror beside the TV and balanced on her left leg. Her right foot pressed against her inner left thigh and knee as she threw her arms over her head, palms together in tree pose. She looked at herself in the mirror to make sure her position was correct, then closed her eyes and focused on her breathing. In through the nose, out through the mouth. Deep controlled breaths. She felt a wave of calm instantly wash over her, the ten-sion of the dream flowing out of her body, down her leg, down the roots of her tree, the roots she imagined grew out of her foot and into the hotel floor.

Then she saw the little girl's screaming face. She lost her bal-ance, put her foot down.

"Fuck," she said, switching legs and trying again.

2

Looking around at her fellow competitors, Julie thought, This is crazy. To her they resembled an army of misfit superheroes, most clad in full black wetsuits, some with goggles that could have been worn by any of a number of caped crusaders.

The woman beside her wore a yellow swimming cap. She was shaking out her arms and legs, gazing out at the water. Julie thought she looked very determined, focused. Julie didn't feel that way. The woman turned her head.

"First Ironman?" she asked.

"Yeah. You?"

"Yeah," she said, giving Julie a smile. Suddenly she felt better, not so alone in a sea of strangers. She could do this.

"I'm Julie."

"Tina," the woman said, extending her hand. They shook.

"Good luck," Tina said, pulling her goggles from her forehead and over her eyes.

"Same to you."

The cannon went off and the water exploded into a churning white froth as close to three thousand competitors scrambled into Okanagan Lake. Julie stayed near the back of the pack to avoid as much of the congestion as possible. Her goal was simply to finish, hopefully in a reasonable time.

When the water reached her knees, she did what everyone else did and dove in. The water was colder than she had expected. She only managed to get two strokes in before she got kicked in the face *twice* by the swimmer in front of her. The blows were quick and powerful and they dislodged her goggles. She thought her nose might be broken. Standing up in the water, now waist deep, she wiped at her nose, checking for blood. Thankfully there was nothing but some snot. After readjusting her goggles she saw Tina's yellow cap twenty metres ahead. Julie dove back in, determined to catch up.

It took twenty minutes before she found a steady rhythm and got into her comfort zone in the water. Never before had she swam with so many people at once. Last night's dream and getting kicked in the face this morning had thrown her off her game. But, as always, Julie quickly recovered. She focused on the mechanics of her swim: her stroke, her kick, her breathing. She knew if she stuck to the basics her form would carry her. Her body lithe in the water, the thrust of her legs becoming more rhythmic, her stroke more fluid and powerful.

Rounding the first large orange buoy, Julie entered the second and shortest leg of the swim. She was only ten metres behind Tina. Julie maintained her rhythmical, fluid stroke. Reach, pull, glide. Reach, pull, glide. Reach, pull, glide. She loved being in her zone, a place of peace, a place where all the world and its problems melted away. As she rounded the second buoy and began the last leg of the swim, she caught up to Tina's yellow cap and started passing her on the outside. Her arms were getting tired and she was looking forward to getting on her bike. In previous races she had thought about her father sitting in the stands watching her. It was usually an image that she tucked away for the end of a race, because it always led her to an angry place. For a few minutes she would be angry with her father, angry with the world, angry with the universe. It would push her, make her go faster, allow her to win. Not today though. Today she thought about her father, envisioned him sitting on a cloud, his arm draped over her mother's shoulder, Luke sitting beside them, all of them smiling, cheering, "Go, Julie!" There was no anger, just an acceptance that they were gone. She didn't believe in heaven or even God for that matter, but she liked to think of them that way, sitting there on a cloud watching her. She found it comforting.

When she exited the water her watch told her she had completed the swimming portion in one hour and ten minutes. She felt this was an acceptable time. She was feeling good, albeit slightly tired. In the transition area she inhaled a gel pack and drank a small amount of water as she changed into her biking garb. Although she couldn't distinguish Ryan in the crowd, she was sure he was there cheering her on. He would be going back to the hotel for a nap and a real breakfast. Eggs and bacon, toast and coffee. She thought about what she would have after the race was over. A steak. A *big* steak. With that tasty image in her head she put on her helmet, unracked her bike and rode off, the crowd cheering her on. Okay, she thought, let's get this done.

Three hours in, heading up a steep hill, Julie's quads burned with lactic acid. A large bead of sweat rolled from under her helmet, down her forehead, past her sunglasses and into her eye. Her eyelid began to spasm and she cursed. She had been following two Australians in bright yellow tops. They had been riding together for over an hour when they broke away from her. She couldn't keep up. Trying to had weakened her. Now she was angry at herself for having pushed too hard too soon. Her goal was to finish, not win. Stick with the plan, slow and steady. This was a long race and a full marathon still remained. There needed to be gas in the tank at the end, not to be wasted now on vanity and pride. Julie hated losing and it was tough for her to watch the Aussies pull away. This was her first Ironman. Next year she could worry about where she was going to place. She focused on the rhythm of her legs rather than the pain. She tried to meditate on her cadence, pushing everything else from her mind. She and the bike were one, a machine, an organic machine. The rhythm, the rhythm, the rhythm. She always ran with music, but the race prohibited all listening devices. It was often Vivaldi's Four Seasons. The open notes of Spring popped into her head and it began to play for her. The violin taking her, carrying her as she pedalled. She could hear it now. The pain in her subsided and she was floating. She hummed it, the rhythm taking her. She was flying, an organic machine.

After the 180 kilometre ride, her legs felt rubbery. She had completed the bike portion four minutes shy of six hours. That was a solid time and she was content with it. She had now been competing for over seven hours, finally entering the last stage of the race, the marathon.

Exiting the transition area for the second time she looked into the crowd. There was Ryan, standing where he said he would be, cheering her on. He had changed his clothes. She knew he would be there. He was dependable, stable. It was these qualities that drew her to him. They had met in university at a friend's Halloween party. She had dressed up as the Paper Bag Princess and Ryan was the only one who got it straight off. He was intelligent, kind, and funny. The thing she liked about him the most was that he gave her space; allowed her to be her. He encouraged her do to the things she loved. He could have stayed home, let her come here by herself. I wouldn't miss it for the all the tea in China, he had said. She gave him a quick wave and a smile and was off running.

After the first five kilometres she was feeling tired, *really* tired. She slowed her pace to a quick walk, grabbed a paper cup of water from a volunteer and drank it down. Then she grabbed another and dumped it over her head. Focus, she told herself, you can do this. Her feet quickened and she broke back into a slow jog. 37 kilometres to go. What was that, seven and a half times the distance she had just run? Piece of cake, she told herself. She grabbed a PowerBar. It tasted of chocolate and peanuts and it was delicious. She was sure she could feel her body instantly absorbing the sugars and carbs, pushing them through her bloodstream with every beat of her heart.

In another five kilometres she had picked up speed and began running with confidence again. She could even take in the beauty of her surroundings. She had seen many of the landmarks in the days prior to the race when she checked out portions of the course. It was a gorgeous day to be running. A new wave of energy was grabbing hold of her. Her legs were on autopilot, moving almost by themselves. Her torso just floated on top enjoying the ride, enjoying the scenery, the hills, Skaha Lake, the crowds of people, everything speeding past like some movie. It was beautiful. Had she ever seen a day like this? And making such great time too. The endorphins were running amok through her brain, and she knew it. She loved this part of exercise. She loved this high. The first time she remembered experiencing such a sense of euphoria was when she was ten. It had been the first time since her brother's death that she had felt great. Once she entered into puberty, the euphoric highs from exercise grew more intense. Everything became more vibrant, colourful, and alive. When her father died, it was how she'd coped. Exercise was the one thing she could always count on to make her happy.

At the run course turnaround, she hit the wall. She'd been swimming, biking and running straight now for over nine and a half hours. She was tired. She was more than tired, she was done. Walking once again, she downed a can of Coke. There were 20 kilometres left. That's only four sets of five kilometres—the quick run she did every morning before work. Easy. Okay, she thought, break it down, do the first run in the morning, do the first run in the morning, do the first run in the morning. Five kilometres. No problem. Here we go. She swung her arms and her feet followed their rhythm. Moving again. Now running again. I'm doing my little morning run, like I always do, she thought. I'm doing it.

The temperature had fallen as the late August sun made its descent toward the horizon. It was halfway through her third "morning run" when her legs turned to Jell-O. Once again she slowed to a walk, and then she stopped. The cramp in her side was intense. She pulled at her flesh with her thumb and forefinger. Other competitors were running by. Somebody yelled that she could do it, someone else bellowed not to give up. Sweat poured down her face. She felt lightheaded. She did a quick mental tally and realized she hadn't taken in enough calories and electrolytes to fuel her through to the end. At the next aid station a volunteer offered her some broth and some pretzels. She grabbed both readily and ingested them as quickly as possible. It didn't take long to kick in. Her cramp began to subside. Two more kilometres, then one final morning run. Seven kilometres total. Come on now, right foot, now the left foot. Good body, good body. Right foot, left foot. Good body. Come on now, we're almost there. Vivaldi's Four Seasons. She hummed Spring. It began to play in her head again. The music was going to carry her in. Right foot, left foot, right foot, left foot. Now we're going. Now we're going.

As she approached the race pavilion the crowds of spectators grew larger. They were cheering on the athletes, cheering her on. She felt their energy, felt it move into her legs, move in through her roots. She was going to finish. Ahead of her she could see the finish line. She was going to make it. Left foot, right foot. Come on body, don't let me down now. It felt like somebody had attached weights to each of her feet, like she was running through thick gooey mud. Each step became its own marathon. Come on, come on, left foot, right foot, left foot, right foot. Come on you bitch, you fucking bitch, you can fucking do this.

Left foot, right foot.

As she crossed the line she heard someone yell, "That one's going down!" And for half a second she wondered who they were talking about. She felt her legs let go. She was falling. Before she landed, two people caught her, placed her in a wheelchair and pushed her towards the medical tent.

★

A handsome medical attendant held her wrist while taking her pulse.

"You're doing well," he said smiling, looking at his watch, "Can you tell me your name?"

"Julie," she sputtered. "Julie Cooper."

"Well, Julie Cooper, can you tell me who the Prime Minister is?"

"Stephen Harper. What was my time?"

"I'm not sure exactly, but you did great. The race officials will have that information for you. You seem to be feeling better."

"Yeah," she said, sitting up straight and sipping a Gatorade, "this is bit embarrassing though."

"Look around," said the medic, "you're not the only one. Be proud. You finished, and in good time."

"Wow," she said, "I did it. I really did it."

4

Across the brown lacquered table sat Ryan holding a glass of sparkling wine.

"Congratulations, baby," he said.

"Thanks for coming with me," Julie said, clinking her glass against his. She was now two hours post-race, showered and changed into a black dress with comfortable sandals.

"I can't believe you just ran an Ironman, and now you're sitting here looking like a goddess."

"You're sweet," she said, draining her glass and immediately feeling lightheaded. She was drunk already.

When the food came—a New York strip loin with a side of garlic mashed potatoes and a Caesar salad—Julie actually salivated. Only in cartoons did she think that happened. She caught the spittle with her napkin before the server or Ryan noticed.

"Go, go," said Ryan, sensing her desire to skip etiquette and eat with unabashed enthusiasm.

She cut into the steak, slicing off a hefty piece. She popped it into her mouth and declared aloud that it might just be better than sex.

"Doubtful," he laughed.

"Oh God it's good," she said as she stuffed another piece into her mouth.

Halfway through her meal she noticed that Ryan had barely touched his.

"What's wrong, aren't you hungry?"

"Just nervous," he said, smiling.

"Nervous about what?"

As she finished asking the question, he slid the small red box across the table. "I was trying to pick the right time to ask. This seems as good as any."

They had been living together for a year now. During their time at university they had seen each other on occasion, but they were both dating other people at the time. They hadn't seen each other for fifteen years until they had run into each other at a coffee shop downtown. It was magical. Electric. They ended up talking for three hours, discussing everything. Like the fact they had both emerged from a series of failed relationships. Ryan had moved around a lot—Thailand, India, Edmonton—before moving back to Ottawa to set up a dental practice with a friend. It was like they both knew at the time that they were with the wrong people, but neither of them had the courage to let go of their life preserver relationships. After dating for only a few months, Ryan had suggested she move in. It had been their first serious fight.

Julie's mother had died of cancer shortly after Julie had completed her Computer Engineering degree. She had been on her own a long time and wasn't ready to let someone take care of her. As much as she liked Ryan, the minute he suggested cohabitating, her walls had gone up. She had "intimacy issues" according to her girlfriend, Sally, who had said it was because of Julie's "fucked up" childhood. Julie didn't think of her childhood as fucked up. Sad, for sure, but never fucked up. Although she couldn't ever fully forgive herself for what happened. And there was a nagging suspicion in Julie's mind that her mother's cancer was brought about by the deaths of her brother and father and the stress of having to raise Julie by herself through her teenage years. Deep down she still took the blame for it all. Ryan, like Sally, had been trying unsuccessfully to convince Julie otherwise. She had agreed to move in with him after almost breaking up over it, as if somehow it would help with her feelings of guilt if she let him in and be part of her life. It didn't help, but she loved him, loved living with him, loved playing house. But now this, a marriage proposal. It was something she had dreamed about as a young girl, but as she grew older the idea seemed more paralyzing. It would make everything real. It wouldn't be playing anymore. All the people she loved went away. She knew that and she knew this was the source of her own reluctance, her "wall" as Sally loved to refer to it.

Ryan was waiting for her to pick up the box. Then she saw a cloud cross his face when she hesitated. It was a look of disappointment. Did she imagine it? It was there for just a second, and then it was gone. She quickly picked up the box and it snapped open like a reverse bear trap. A red stone shone in the centre of a silver Celtic lattice band with three teardrop diamonds running down each side. It wasn't a typical engagement ring. It was a unique and beautiful ring and it confirmed her deep feelings for Ryan. He wouldn't buy a big flashy diamond because he wasn't that kind of man and, more importantly, she wasn't that kind of woman. He understood that about her. That's why she loved him so much.

"Yes," she said.

"I didn't even ask you yet," he said, breaking into a laugh.

"It's gorgeous," she said, slipping the ring onto her finger.

Ryan didn't say anything. He just smiled instead.

"Why now?" she asked.

"What?"

"Why now? Why did you ask me now?" And as soon as the words left her mouth she wished she could retract them. It wasn't really the words she said, but how she said them. They held a kind of accusatory tone that behind this marriage proposal there must be an ulterior motive.

"Well I just thought it was time. I mean you're going to be 38 this year and I thought you might want to have kids," he said.

And there it was. She pulled it out of him just like that.

"So you want to marry me because you want to have kids?" she asked with the same tone, and once again wished she could take it back, but she was unable to stop herself.

"I just thought we were heading in that direction."

"I don't know if I'm ready for that. I was hoping to come back here next year, improve my time."

"I know, but if we're going to have kids, we should do it soon."

"How do you even know if I want fucking kids?"

The light drained from his eyes. Her walls had gone up and she needed to bring them down quickly.

"I thought you said you did? Look, I'm sorry . . ."

"No," she said, cutting him off, "I'm sorry. I don't know what's wrong with me sometimes. I'm just really tired. Listen, Ryan, the ring is beautiful and I'll marry you and it'll be great. I just have that problem with personal space as you know, and I'm trying to work through it and I'm sorry."

"I know, Julie, it's okay," he said, breaking back into a smile.

"I love you, you know," she said.

"I know."

★

It was late and the last of the runners were still trickling in. Julie thought about them as she and Ryan walked into the neon light of the tattoo parlour. A young girl, maybe twenty, was sitting at a coffee table flipping through a binder of unicorns and teddy bears while her friend lay on a table. She grimaced slightly as the muscular man with surgical gloves wiped the blood from her lower back. The "tramp stamp," thought Julie. Amazing. The buzz of the needle grew louder as another man, older, with a beard and greying hair pulled back into a braid, came walking over to them with a slight limp. His arms were covered in comic book women and angry looking dragons.

"Let me guess. Ironman tattoo?" he said.

"How'd you know?" Julie asked.

"You're the third one tonight. Besides, you look like an athlete. You can tell a lot about a person from their veins," he said. She couldn't tell if he was smiling, his beard was so thick, but she thought he might be.

"Yes. Right here on the ankle please."

"Well, let me show you what it'll look like," he said, waddling behind his counter.

The leaves of the trees had by now changed colour, and most were already half bare. A shower of honey mustard leaves blew off a large maple in the crisp October morning wind, and Julie ran through them as she jogged alongside Ottawa's canal. It was Saturday. That meant an easy 25 kilometres. She was only 10 kilometres in when a wave of nausea hit her. She shook her head, kept running. Funny, what had she eaten? Nothing odd. Then it came again, this time with more intensity. She stopped by a tree and leaned on it for support while she threw up on the grass. Then the thought entered her mind: she was late. Her period was supposed to have arrived two weeks ago.

After she was sick she felt much better and continued running, but then suddenly made a detour up to Bank Street.

Now seated in the public washroom of the Shoppers Drug Mart, Julie pulled the plastic stick from between her legs and stared at the little oval window next to the embossed stork.

"Come on, come on," she said aloud.

A faint purple line appeared, and then grew darker.

"Fuck," she said. "Fuck, fuck, fuck."

"Pass me the wipes," Julie said. Ryan did, and she shoved the plastic box into the diaper bag.

"How are you feeling? Are you sure you're up for this?" he asked.

If she were honest, she would say no, not at all. She felt fat. She had run all the way up to the eight month mark. However, during the last trimester of her pregnancy, she had been unable to reach the high of exercise she normally obtained. A month after she had given birth she was still holding onto an extra 15 pounds of pregnancy weight. Sally, who'd had three kids, had told her to stuff a sock in it; she looked incredible. Julie wasn't worried so much about how she looked as how she felt. She hadn't felt good since the baby was born. She wasn't sure she was bonding with Kayla as she should be. There had been trouble with breastfeeding and her nipples remained bruised and raw. Depression had been coming in slow waves: random bouts of crying while watching afternoon TV game shows; fatigue of epic proportions; even thoughts of running away, getting on a bus and just leaving. Sally called it the baby blues, said most mothers went through it. She said not to worry, that it would get better. This was going to be Julie's first run since Kayla was born. She needed it desperately, craved that physical high that exercise gave her.

Julie placed little Kayla in her car seat inside her new three-wheeled Chariot running stroller. After buckling her in she stood up and her boobs felt enormous. Normally she was a B cup at best, but now she was pushing the limits of the C cup. Porn star boobs, Ryan called them. Sex was the furthest thing from her mind.

"I'm good to go," she said smiling, trying to convince both him and herself of that fact. She didn't think he believed her and she didn't really believe it herself, but you had to start somewhere. Going out the door, that was the first step. Step by step she was going to run herself back to her pre-baby body, run herself mentally and physically back to health. When she ran regularly, everything else in her life fell easily, naturally, into place. She kissed him on the cheek and went out the door.

★

Julie thought the trees looked pregnant. That thought had never crossed her mind before. Pregnant trees. It was those full, dark green leaves, swollen and big. The trees looked tired. It had been a hot summer and now, in mid August, the trees looked like they'd had enough, like they wanted to shed their leaves and be done with this oppressive heat. It was already 21 degrees and not even 9:00AM. The forecast for the week was the same as it had been all summer: hot. The whole province had been sweltering under a heat wave and it wasn't letting up any time soon.

Two kilometres into it, Julie had already broken into a good hard sweat. Her muscles ached. She stopped to make sure Kayla was breathing as she hadn't heard a peep from her. Still sleeping soundly. Sip of water, then back at it.

At the five kilometre mark she was feeling good, awash in endorphins. This was her bliss. Then she noticed her shirt was wet. She had lactated through her bra, milk soaking two large circles into the front of her shirt. As she looked up to see where she was going, two men came jogging toward her. She caught it. The man on the far left was pulling back his hand, his chin thrust forward. Pulling it back from pointing, or maybe it was just a nudge. "Check it out," he was probably saying. His friend turned his head, followed the direction of his chin, to stare at Julie's tits, her swollen lactating tits. And did that man snicker as they went by?

"Fuck you," she yelled out. It wasn't a vicious fuck you, but merely a self-deprecating "Yes I know I look like shit, so fuck you," kind of fuck you. She heard them laugh as they continued to run in the other direction. Kayla let out a cry. Julie stopped at the next bench along the pathway and fed her. She was changing her diaper when her phone rang.

"Everything okay?" Ryan asked. His voice didn't betray any sense of real worry, something that might have said, "Just checking you didn't jump off a bridge with my baby." No, nothing like that. Ryan was merely being Ryan. Sweet and kind. He would never point and laugh at some woman's squirting tits. Well, he might, but he wouldn't be so unsubtle about it.

"Had to stop and feed Kayla. My tits are leaking all over the fucking place. I'm heading home in a minute. I'm out of shape."

"I'm sure you're doing great," he said.

"It's nice to be out again."

"Good. I was thinking maybe we could even go out for dinner if you're up for it?"

"Well, I . . . yes. Let's try it."

"Good. See you two soon."

"Love you," she said. He repeated the words and hung up.

The idea of going out yesterday would have been unimaginable, but today, now, how could they not go out? How wonderful did she feel? All she needed was to run. She had poured half her water bottle onto her shirt so as to hide the mess of her dribbling breasts. Now she just looked a sweaty mess. A fabulously sweaty mess. Running, moving, free. Her legs were once again moving on their own. This is what she needed. A large smile broke across her face. Oh what bliss this was. She would shower and put on that black dress, the one she wore after her Ironman, the one she wore when Ryan proposed. Hmm, might not fit. Not to worry, she would find something. The trees no longer looked pregnant, but rather full of life, full of energy. Her legs were plugged into that energy, feeding off it. Yes, she would be the mother she wanted to be; all she had to do was run. All the way home she thought about writing an article about running and new moms. A firsthand, personal account of how running could save you.

She opened the front door and pushed the stroller through. Kayla was awake but unperturbed, happily inspecting the black and white toys dangling from the canopy. Julie moved into the hall where Ryan stood with the portable phone in hand.

"What's wrong?" she asked, noting the expression on his face.

"That was your Aunt Jennie."

"And?"

"Uncle Simon died."

"Oh no," she said. "When? How?"

"This morning. Heart attack."

7

The plane was much smaller than Julie had anticipated, a claustrophobic tube. Only two single rows of seats separated by a narrow aisle. Maximum capacity: 19 people. This was not the plane in her dream, and because of that her anxiety was slightly diminished.

The choice to fly to North Bay hadn't been an easy one, but she didn't feel comfortable driving with Kayla such a long distance without Ryan just yet, and the idea of the bus, well, she hated it more than the plane. The bus gave her motion sickness. So flying it was. Ryan, being Ryan, was sweet and of course offered to drive her to the funeral, but his business partner was already on vacation that week and he was doing double duty trying to keep up with the extra workload. He would have had to cancel a ton of clients. She insisted she'd be fine; Aunt Jennie would pick her up from the airport.

The flight attendant came over and gave Julie instructions on what to do if there was an emergency landing, how she was to hold Kayla. "Cradle her like this," she said. Julie thought about the movie *Fearless* with Jeff Bridges, about that scene in which he intentionally drove his car into a wall with Rosie Perez holding a metal toolbox. She let go of the box, which represented her baby, the one she let go of when her plane crashed. Jeff Bridges was proving a point: you couldn't have held on to your baby during the plane crash, it was impossible; laws of physics; it's not your fault.

Julie smiled at the attendant and wished she had taken the bus after all.

As soon as the plane left the ground, Kayla began to wail. The plane was only three quarters full. A teenage boy sat across the aisle from her reading a Stephen King novel, ear buds in his ears.

The prop engines were so loud she wondered if anyone else besides her could even hear Kayla's cries. Julie lifted her shirt and undid her nursing bra and latched Kayla onto her nipple. Julie caught the boy checking her out. He quickly turned away. Men and boobs, ridiculous, she thought.

She nursed Kayla for 15 minutes and then she dozed off. Julie thought about poor Aunt Jennie. She was Julie's mother's older sister. There had been an almost 10-year age gap between the two. Julie's mother Edie would have turned 68 next week if she was still alive. Despite the distance and age difference, Aunt Jennie and Edie had always been close. Julie remembered her aunt coming to stay with her those last few weeks her mom was being devoured by cancer. Aunt Jennie had always been good to her, always sending Christmas gifts and birthday cards stuffed with twenty dollar bills. Julie was spoiled by her aunt and uncle and knew it. She always assumed it was because they could never have kids of their own. Before Kayla showed up, they had sent a cheque for five thousand dollars to cover all the "little things," as it had said in the card. It was close to three years since the last time she had seen them, and as the wheels touched down a wave of guilt washed over her for not being a better niece. She should have called more, visited more. And now here she was, ready to bury her uncle, the closest thing she'd had to a father since she was a teen.

Julie saw her aunt waving through the window as she walked across the hot tarmac towards the terminal. Kayla was crying again and Julie suspected she needed changing.

Rounding the corner and walking through the door, Julie saw her. She looked as if she had aged far more than three years. She had lost weight, her wrinkles were far more pronounced, and her posture wilted. She looked as she was—old, frail, and very sad. Julie burst into tears and gave her aunt a hug, though not as hard as she would have liked, worried she might snap her like a twig. Her aunt squeezed back with more force than Julie expected and this made her happy. She was a tough old girl, her aunt. She'd been through her own bout with cancer and won.

"Sorry, Aunt Jennie," Julie said, wiping her eyes.

"That's alright, dear, he's in a better place now. He hadn't been well for the last year, you know. It's too bad you didn't get to say goodbye. Simon always thought of you as his daughter."

A fresh wave of guilt crashed over Julie. How could she have been so selfish?

"I'm so sorry, I should have come to see you last year. Just with everything, my training, and then the pregnancy . . . Still, it's no excuse."

"Oh my God, let me see her," said Jennie, pulling a crying Kayla from Julie's arms.

"She needs to be changed I think."

"I'll do it," she said. "Give me the diaper stuff."

"Are you sure?"

"Listen, dear, I may be a little old lady, but I can still change a diaper."

"Okay, why don't we do it together," Julie said, worried her aunt might drop Kayla by accident.

★

After they collected Julie's luggage and Kayla's stroller, they headed outside the Jack Garland Airport. There were only a half dozen cars in the parking lot but Jennie seemed confused.

"What's wrong, forget where you parked?" Julie joked.

"Well that's just it, I don't know where my car is," Jennie said, shading her eyes with her hand while she scanned the near empty parking lot.

"Maybe it was stolen? Should we go back in and report it?"

"Radios maybe, but who steals cars in North Bay besides the Quinton boys?" Jennie said.

"Well, it's got to be one of those then, right?"

"I don't know," Jennie said, growing increasingly agitated and confused. She held out her car keys and pressed the fob. The black Chrysler 300, the car parked closest to them in the handicapped stall, let out a high pitched electronic chirp and flashed its lights.

"Is that it right there?" asked Julie, pointing.

"Oh how embarrassing. Don't know what's wrong with me. I was looking for our old station wagon. It's no fun getting old," Jennie said, smiling again.

As they walked to the car, Julie knew it wasn't something she could fix, something she could help her aunt with. Her mind was going and Julie knew she would likely end up in a home like her grandfather. He'd had Alzheimer's. She remembered visiting him in the hospital. He was kept in thick beige restraints so he couldn't claw at his own flesh. He would scream out every once in a while as if he was in horrible pain. She hated going. She thought of her poor aunt possibly having to go through something similar. Now, with her uncle gone, Jennie was bound to deteriorate quickly. Julie had to get through the next few days—help with the funeral, help her aunt close up the cottage, help with all the paperwork, death certificates and bank accounts and so on. But she knew, after it was all over, she would need to return, maybe even within a month to make sure her aunt was looked after.

8

The church was big and the pews were almost full. Julie recognized a few of her uncle and aunt's friends. Reverend Marshal did a fine job and kept the service light on religion, for which Julie was grateful. Jennie clutched Julie's hand the entire time, stoically not shedding a tear until they moved to the cemetery. It wasn't until they lowered her husband of fifty years into the ground that she let go. Even then, though, Julie's aunt wasn't a blubbery mess, wailing like she could have, like some people might have. Julie hoped this strength of character ran in her gene pool. She was proud of her aunt, impressed by how she carried on considering how feeble she looked.

There was a reception afterwards in the church's basement. Little old ladies who resembled her aunt dished out platters of triangular sandwiches on white bread with the crusts cut off and pots of lousy coffee. One person after the next came to pay their respects to Jennie and introduce themselves to Julie. "Oh, you must be Julie." "Oh, yes, Julie, I've heard so much about you. So sorry about your uncle." "Julie, oh, you're the athlete. I heard you almost went to the Olympics."

"Almost, but didn't," Julie said, trying her best to keep smiling. It had been three years following her father's death when she finished just shy of making the swim team for the 1992 Barcelona summer Olympics. She stopped swimming competitively after that, only hitting the water recreationally at the beach or at a friend's cottage. It would be fourteen years before she once again entered the water with a competitive spirit, when she began to train for her first Ironman.

"Oh you're, Julie," said the next little old lady in the series, "You won't remember me, but I met you when you were just a young girl, and now look at you. All grown up with a child of your own. Why, isn't she the prettiest little angel? Oh my, how precious is she. Wonderful. I'm Betty," she said, shaking Julie's hand, "a very old friend of Simon and Jennie." Betty leaned in close to Julie when her aunt was busy talking with someone else.

"I don't know how much you know about your aunt's situation, dear, but Simon had been really working hard at keeping the ship afloat, if you know what I mean."

"No, I'm not sure I do know what you mean."

"Your aunt, well she's not well in her mind. Forgetful. He told me that one morning she woke up and didn't know who he was. Screamed at him, asked him who he was. She wanted to know who this complete stranger was in her house. He tried to convince her that he was Simon, but she wouldn't listen. He went about his day, as he normally would. Every time he came near her she would threaten to call the police, tell him to get out of her house. He went outside, cut the lawn, and then went to church. He said he didn't know what to do. Then he prayed. He was worried that he shouldn't have left her by herself, so halfway through the service, he left. He pulled into the driveway and Jennie said, 'Oh there you are, thank God. There's been a stranger in the house.' Ask her about it if you like, she still talks about it, the time when Simon left her alone in the house with a strange man. Anyway, I wanted to tell you because I think Jennie is going to need some care, if you know what I mean."

"I didn't know it was that bad. Thanks for telling me."

"I'll give you my number if you like."

"Yes, thank you."

Julie looked over at her aunt who was smiling and shaking hands as if everything was completely normal. Julie knew it wasn't.

★

That night the dream returned. The screams of the mother yelling "Save her!" morphed into the cries of Kayla lying in the queensized bed beside her. Julie fed her, changed her, rocked her and Kayla continued to cry. Julie repeated the sequence. Kayla continued to howl. Aunt Jennie poked her head into Julie's room.

"Not settling down is she?"

"No," said Julie. She was exhausted, and in the morning they were going to go to the cottage to close it up for the season. "Maybe I'll try feeding her again."

"Want me to try rocking her for a bit?"

Normally Julie wouldn't have let her aunt—frail, three days widowed, and in a questionable mental state—take her baby from her. No, normally she would have sent her back to bed. But the fatigue of caring for a newborn was finally catching up. Ryan was a good father, taking more than his share of middle of the night changes, but Julie was the only one who could breastfeed and she felt she hadn't had a proper sleep since Kayla was born. Exhausted and with tomorrow's trip to the cottage looming, Julie handed Kayla over. Even though her aunt never had children of her own, instinct took over as Jennie rocked and shushed Kayla. Within two minutes Jennie had lulled her to sleep.

"Look at you, the baby whisperer," said Julie.

"I rocked you to sleep a few times when you were this size," said Jennie, smiling.

"I wish my mom was here to see her."

"Me too, dear," Jennie said, laying Kayla back on the bed. "You try and get some sleep now and I'll see you in the morning."

"Thanks, Aunt Jennie, you're a life saver."

"Now, if I could only remember where my bedroom was?"

"Oh," said Julie, the surprise in her voice evident.

"Just messing with you. I know my old brain is going in the toilet, but I know where my bedroom is. At least for now I do. Goodnight child."

"Not funny, Aunt Jennie," said Julie with a playful scolding finger wag.

"Goodnight."

★

Julie went back to sleep, went back to her dream. A little girl with bleached, straw-blonde hair was running down the aisle of the plane. She looked so happy.

9

With a head of lettuce, a cucumber and a tomato in her hands, Julie slowed as she approached her aunt standing in the meat department of Sobey's. She was flipping the red plastic children's seat guard slowly up and down. It appeared that she was confused by it, as if she was trying to figure out how it worked.

"You okay, Aunt Jennie?" asked Julie, placing the veggies into the cart next to the car seat in which Kayla was sleeping.

"Oh, this damn thing, I can't remember if it's supposed to go up or down," Jennie said, her voice clearly agitated as she continued to flick the plastic tab.

"Doesn't really matter," said Julie, coming to her aunt's rescue. Julie softly placed her hands over her aunt's. "Why don't we leave it up and we can put a couple of steaks in there?"

"Okay," said Jennie, looking up. Julie thought her aunt was going to cry.

"It's fine, Aunt Jennie. You're okay. Let's get those steaks, shall we?"

Jennie nodded.

★

Waiting in line at the checkout, Kayla woke up crying. Julie changed her in the Sobeys' bathroom, then breastfed her in the back of the Chrysler in the parking lot. She left the door wide open until the air conditioner was running full blast. It was 10:00AM and already over thirty degrees with the humidex. Julie couldn't wait to take a swim. They were going to the cottage she used to visit when she was a child. It was the reason her parents had bought theirs. It was the reason neither she nor her parents had ever returned.

After loading the groceries into the cooler, Julie buckled Kayla into her car seat. Julie gave her a light kiss on the top of her head while she tucked a light blanket around her.

"Are you sure you don't want me to drive?" asked Julie.

"I'm fine, dear. Why don't you close your eyes and have a little nap. It's only a forty minute drive."

"I'm okay. You must be tired too, after the funeral and everything."

"I'm fine. It's just hard going up because Simon loved the camp so much."

Julie didn't say anything. She grabbed her aunt and gave her a big hug.

"Aren't you going to be hot in that?" asked Julie, letting her go. Her aunt was wearing a white blouse with a purple silk scarf and beige slacks.

"It's all cotton, dear. I'll be fine. Let's go."

The car ride was a smooth one and Julie's eyes felt heavy. She let the lull of the car take her to sleep.

It was the transition to the rumbling, popping sounds of the tires on a gravel road that stirred her awake again. They were off the highway, driving through the forest, the sun directly overhead.

"Have a good rest?" asked her aunt.

"Yeah, that was lovely," said Julie, sitting up and stretching her arm. Kayla was still sleeping. Life was good. Then Julie noticed the clock. 11:40. She looked at the gas gauge. The needle was creeping dangerously close to empty.

"Shouldn't we be there by now?"

"Should be there any minute," said her aunt, smiling.

"Thought it was a forty minute drive?"

"It is. Sometimes Simon would do it in thirty if he pushed it."

"Well, it's been an hour and a half, Aunt Jennie," said Julie, the tone of her voice echoing the anxiety she was feeling.

"Oh, no, has it been that long?"

"We left the parking lot shortly after ten."

"Oh, maybe I took a wrong turn?"

"Maybe we should turn around. The gas is getting low."

"I'm sure it's just up here," Jennie said with confidence in her voice, a confidence Julie found surprising and disturbing. Maybe it took longer to get there than she said?

"You said it took forty minutes. Did you mean an hour and forty minutes?"

"No, no, forty minutes. Forty five at most," said Jennie, smiling like nothing was wrong.

"Aunt Jennie, we need to turn around I think," Julie said, noticing the road had narrowed to a single lane, the ground becoming extremely bumpy. Unkempt.

"Now, now, don't worry, we're almost there. I'm going to have to call Dennis and have him fix up this road. It's never been this bad before."

The car bounced up and down wildly over the rough terrain. Branches of trees and bushes scraped the car windows like a carwash. Julie braced herself against the dashboard as they continued to spring and roll along. She expected Kayla to wake any minute.

The foliage cleared and they rolled out into a tall grassy field. The road ended and Jennie brought the car to a stop.

"What's going on? Are we here?" asked Julie.

"This is wrong, this is all wrong," murmured Jennie, shaking her head, looking puzzled at the sight before her, a rocky and vast landscape. Raw and beautiful, but without a lake or a cottage.

"Are we lost?"

"I don't understand, it should be right here," said Jennie. Julie cursed under her breath. She shouldn't have let her aunt drive. Why had she done that? It was her fault as much as it was her aunt's. Julie looked over and the gas needle was resting on top of the E.

"We'd better turn around, Aunt Jennie. We're getting close to running out of gas. We can try again after we fill up."

"It should be right here. I must have made a wrong turn," Jennie said, finally turning to look at Julie. "I'm sorry."

"It's okay, we'll just turn around and go back the way we came."

"Okay," said Jennie, turning the wheel to the left and driving the car into the tall bleached grass. She shifted the car into reverse and shot back. There was a large bump accompanied by a loud noise, like somebody had popped a paper bag inside the car. Julie thought, Shit.

"Oh, no," said Jennie.

"Think that was the tire. I'll check," said Julie, unbuckling her seatbelt. As she opened the door she was immediately over-whelmed by the contrasting heat. Fuck, it's going to be a bitch changing a tire in this goddamn heat, she thought. Sure enough, the tire was flat. Aunt Jennie had run over some rusty piece of farm equipment, possibly a tractor grate. Shit. The car emitted an electronic dinging as Jennie opened her door. She shuffled around and stood by her niece to survey the damage.

"Oh my, look at that," said Jennie.

"I'll have to put the spare on. Drive back over that first and park it, then I'll change it."

"Oh, I'm so sorry, Julie."

"It's okay, accidents happen."

Jennie shuffled back to the driver's door and pulled on the handle. The car was still running.

"Oh, silly me, I've locked myself out. Try yours."

Julie pulled on the back door where Kayla was. Locked. She pulled on her door. Locked. She went around and tried the others. Both locked. All locked. Shit.

"Well unless you have a spare key, looks like we'll have to bust the window."

Jennie looked at her niece and shook her head.

"It's okay, Aunt Jennie, we'll get it fixed. I promise, okay?"

"No my dear, you can't."

"Well we have to." Julie's voice rose in volume and agitation, "Now don't we?"

"No, you don't understand. You *can't*."

"What do you mean I 'can't'?"

"Your uncle, he was worried about the stereo system he had installed in the car. He loved listening to John Coltrane and . . . now who was it . . . Anyway," she said, "because his friend Bernie had his car radio stolen, your uncle went and got this shatterproof coating put on the windows. He told me you'd need a wrecking ball to break them."

Julie ran her hand through her hair. She turned her head and looked at Kayla still sleeping in the backseat. Something needed to be done and quickly.

"Well, we're going to have to try," said Julie. "Help me look for a rock."

Julie quickly found a baseball-sized piece of granite. "Got one," she said. She walked around to the passenger's window and cocked back her arm. She looked at her aunt standing at the front of the car. A bead of sweat rolled down Julie's back as she swung the stone. It bounced off the window like rubber. Julie swung again, this time with more force, and the impact reverberated up her arm. Nothing. She looked closely at the window. Not even a nick or a scratch. She swung again, this time not holding anything back. It felt like she had punched a wall. She swung again. And again. Nothing.

"We need a bigger rock," Julie stated, and immediately went looking for one. It was near the edge of the forest that she found one partially embedded in the dirt. Barely able to lift it from the ground, Julie walked with the rock ape-like. She held it dangling down in front of her, her hands locked under it, resting it against her crotch and thighs. When she got to the car she couldn't hold it anymore and let the rock slip down, scraping both legs as it went. Tiny droplets of blood beaded along the long scrape on her left leg.

"Fuck," she sighed, her face and arms glistening with perspiration.

"Oh my, be careful, my dear," said Jennie. Julie didn't say anything. She took a minute, catching her breath. She looked at the window. She visualized the rock smashing through it, landing on the seat. "Okay," she said, picking it up again, this time lifting it to her chest. At five feet away, she stepped once, twice, and launched the rock. It hit the window exactly where she intended it to, dead centre. The rock rolled down the side of the car scratching the paint as it went. Julie couldn't believe it.

"Are you fucking kidding me?" she said, hoisting it up again. And again she hit the window and it rolled off. This time she slipped in her flip-flop sandals and didn't get out of the way as the

rock fell on the toes of her right foot. Julie let out a cry and fell
to the ground, clutching her foot.

Jennie came running to her side. "Are you okay?"

"I think I broke a couple of toes, maybe worse," she said,
grimacing.

"Oh no. What are we going to do?"

"Help me up," she ordered. It's then they heard Kayla let out
a cry from the back seat. Julie pressed up against the glass. "It's
okay, baby. Mommy's going to get you out in a second."

When she pulled herself off the car, her aunt saw Julie's eyes.
They were the eyes of a trapped animal. She limped over and
picked up the baseball-sized rock again. She screamed and hit the
window. It was a howling scream full of fear and anger. She did
it again and again and again, and each time she screamed her aunt
winced. Julie beat against the window fifteen times with everything she had, and on the sixteenth attempt her sweat-soaked
palm slipped off the stone. Her fist hit the glass, breaking the
fourth and fifth metacarpal bones of her hand. The pain shot up
her arm, resonated like a gong in her elbow, and continued all the
way to her shoulder. Julie saw a flash of light and fell back, her
mouth agape in agony. Tears fell from her eyes. She cradled her
arm and thought she was going to be sick. She tasted bile in her
mouth.

"Are you okay?"

"I broke it," she said in a soft whimper, "I broke it. My foot
and my hand, I broke them."

Kayla was still crying, the sound muted by the car engine.
Julie hopped over and looked through the driver's window at the
gas gauge. It rested on top of the E. She knew she didn't have
much time. Think, think, think. The diamonds on her engagement ring could cut the glass. Damn it—no ring. She remembered taking it off in the last month of pregnancy when her fingers had swollen up. She never put it back on. Aunt Jennie only
wore a gold band. Julie looked around for anything. There were
no telephone poles, no wires, no indication they were near anyone with a phone. However, there was this old piece of farm
equipment. It meant someone had been here. They couldn't be

that far from someone. If they drove an extra hour at 50 KPH, then they were only 50 kilometres off track theoretically. She looked down at her broken foot and saw the little Ironman tattoo on her ankle. Less than a year ago she had completed an Ironman, she told herself. You can do this. She turned to her aunt.

"I'm going for help," said Julie, pulling off her T-shirt. "Help me rip this into pieces. I need to sling my arm and tie my flip-flops to my feet."

10

Every step hurt. Pain shot up her right leg and arm as she limped along, and her foot and hand were both ballooning. She had made it back to the point where the road widened to two lanes. She didn't know how long she had been running. She guessed twenty minutes, but wasn't sure. She was thirsty. Each bird that chirped reminded her of Kayla crying in that car. Hurry up. Come on, come on. Julie didn't see the branch jutting out onto the road from a fallen tree. The shirt fabric she used to securely fasten her flip-flops snagged it and with the help of a pothole sent her tumbling to the road. She managed to scrape the palm of her good hand as well as her chin and both knees. She got back to her feet, re-tied her sandal as best she could, readjusted her sling, and was off again.

The sun was directly above her. It's heat was relentless and there was no shade on the road. The forest echoed with the noise of the crickets, an almost electric sound, which began with a low pitched hum and rose to a maddening, crescendoing buzz. It was like the sun itself was making the noise. The sound of a heat lamp turned on full blast.

Her bra was soaked through, as were her underwear and shorts. She didn't let her mind wander off to what was happening. Instead she focused on the run, focused on finishing and getting help.

She tripped on a rock and fell, sprawling out, landing hard. The taste of dirt and blood filled her mouth. She lay there for a minute, catching her breath. She sat up and spit. A gooey tendril of red dangled from her chin as she screamed, "Help!" She screamed it over and over. A few minutes later she stopped, stood up, wiped the spittle from her face, and began to run again. When she reached a T in the road she didn't know what to do. There were no signs, no indication which way led to the highway. She wanted to go south, but the sun wasn't offering any intimation of where that might be. She went right for no other reason than it felt right. It was a decision, but good or bad she didn't know. It was a decision she made and would have to live with if it was wrong.

★

The road flattened and straightened out. A deer stepped out of the woods fifteen feet in front of her. They both stopped. The deer turned its head to look at Julie. Its ears seemed to move independently; little radar dishes spinning about the top of the animal's head. It didn't seem afraid. It looked upon Julie with curiosity; why are you way out here? It turned its head back and slowly crossed the road, disappearing into the bush. She began to run again. She thought about her brother struggling in the water. Did he try to call for help? Did he call for help but she hadn't heard him because she was so focused on winning?

"I'm sorry, Luke," she said, and began to hum Vivaldi.

The music began to play in her head. It grew louder and more intense. Then her mind went where she didn't want it to. It went to Kayla in the car. It went to Ryan's face. Her legs began to move faster. Then she heard it, coming from behind: an engine, and tires on the road. She turned around and saw the front of a pickup truck round the corner. She stood in the middle of the road waving her left arm back and forth above her head. The truck was moving quickly, not slowing down.

"Help me! Please, help . . ."

The truck veered hard to the right. She felt the powerful gush of air as it zoomed by, missing her only by inches. The sounds of heavy metal blaring from inside the cabin dissipated as she watched it pull away and disappear around the next bend.

Aghast, she began to run again. How long had she been running? An hour? She focused on her left arm, her good arm, moving it back and forth. Moving her arm moved her feet. She thought of herself as a child's wooden toy: you pull the string and its arms and legs fly out together. Move the arm, move the legs. Move the arm, move the legs.

Another T in the road appeared ahead, and as she approached it she heard the sounds of another vehicle. She was disoriented, dehydrated, and couldn't tell from which direction the sound emanated. She spun around. It was coming closer. And finally there it was, a blue minivan.

"Help me!" she screamed, running toward the intersection. She saw the face of the driver, saw him actually look at her as he drove past. A cloud of dust rolled up behind. Julie thought, How could they not stop? How on earth could they see me and not stop? And then through the ghostly cloud appeared the red eyes of the taillights.

She ran. The car door opened and a man stepped out.

"Are you okay?"

"Help me," she panted. "Please, my baby." Her vision became spotted. Grey. Then everything turned an inky black.

PART 2
MEDICATION

The angry squawk of a crow outside her window awoke her. Julie opened her eyes. The digital clock surrounded by pill bottles told her it was almost noon. The skin on her upper forearm under the cast was itchy. It felt like a red ant attack. She grabbed her wooden chopstick off the nightstand and worked it under the blue fibreglass. Relief. She grabbed three of the little amber jars of medication and popped one lid after the next, taking a pill from each. She sat up and looked at the pills in her hand. She got up, walked to the bathroom and sucked them back. Her pale reflection greeted her in the mirror. She was appalled at her bloodshot eyes and accompanying dark circles. A miniature tornado had evidently ripped through her hair during the night, leaving a tangled mess behind. She sat on the toilet and peed, after which she staggered back to bed.

Julie opened her eyes. The digital clock read 3:14. She sat up. Her mouth was dry and her brain felt heavy, hazy, dull. "Fuck," she said. She had missed her 2:00PM doctor's appointment to get her cast removed. After making a call, she had a quick shower with her arm thrust out of the stall. Her toothbrush in her mouth felt foreign. There was hardly any saliva when she spit. She sucked on the tap, but even then her mouth still felt dry.

As she walked by the closed door of Kayla's room, she paused. Stale air greeted her as she swung open the door. A bookcase sat in the corner of the room holding a variety of items: a pink teddy bear, a musical snow globe, a few children's books, wooden toys, and some framed pictures. On the top shelf sat the rock, her brother's rock. She picked it up and rubbed it against her cheek. It was as smooth as the day they had found it. A photo of Ryan stared at her from the bookshelf. Fat wooden letters were glued to the bottom of the frame spelling out DAD. He looked so happy. And there on the other side of the same shelf, a photo of Julie, with matching MOM letters. She threw the rock at her own photo; it hit the frame and ricocheted back, sending the photo crashing to the ground. The glass shattered and one of the Ms broke off and spun across the floor. She picked up the rock again and placed it in Kayla's crib.

"So sorry, baby," she said rubbing her hand against the soft cotton of the crib sheet. "Mommy loves you forever."

2

Dr. Chan watched Julie slowly open and close her hand, unable to fully extend or contract it.

"How's it feel?" he asked.

"Weak, stiff, like I just got a cast off," she replied with a smile.

"That's normal," he said. "But no pain, correct?"

"Correct."

"Well it looks nicely healed. I'm going to have you see a physiotherapist, okay?"

"Okay," she said as she watched him key something into his computer. A moment later his printer spit out a piece of paper.

"Here's the referral for the physio. There's a list of several places you can go to at the bottom. Your choice, or you can find others."

"Thanks," she said, standing up to leave.

"Look, before you go. How are you doing *mentally*?"

Mentally. He said it as if it was something clandestine, like it was something to be embarrassed about. Your drunk uncle at Christmas being too loud, saying inappropriate things.

"It's rough. I won't lie," she answered, the smile fading back to the dull shape of a medicated mouth; not a frown, just a mouth, like a doll's.

"Are you seeing anyone?"

"I'm engaged to be married," she said as her eyebrows crinkled puzzlement.

Dr. Chan smiled awkwardly. "Ah, no. I mean, are you seeing a counsellor, or a therapist, or even a support group?"

She shook her head. "My fiancé, Ryan, he wanted me to join a grieving group, but those things aren't for me."

"Well if a group isn't your thing, maybe a one-on-one with somebody might be good for you. The death of a child is one of the hardest things anybody can go through."

"Have you lost a child?" she snapped and immediately regretted doing so. She understood he was only trying to help. She didn't want to be *that* person, that angry person. Before he could answer she said, "Sorry, never mind. I haven't been sleeping well."

"It's okay, it's understandable," he said.

"It's not that," she said. "I've been having these dreams, nightmares really. They've been getting worse."

"Listen, here is the name of a friend of mine, a psychiatrist, Dr. Bell," he said, scribbling a number on a script pad. "He's not currently accepting new patients, but I'll call in a favour and get him to see you. That is, if you like."

"I'm okay," she said.

"Please, take his number, just in case you change your mind," he said, offering it to her.

"Okay, thanks," she said.

On the way to the car she crumpled the piece of paper and threw it in the trash.

★

Ryan and his partner closed the office early on Fridays, so Julie was surprised to see Mona and Jill's cars still there. When she walked into the lobby, she saw a long dark coat hanging on the hook and a pair of glossy men's shoes on the matt. Mona looked up from across the sitting room and waved from behind the reception desk.

"Hi, Julie," she said. "Guy broke his crown chewing a pen at work. He's flying off tonight on a business trip, so Ryan said he'd fix it."

That was just so Ryan, always willing to help out and do that little bit extra. A good man, Julie thought.

"I came to pick him up, show him this," she said, holding up her arm. It felt strange holding it aloft, light and scrawny, the weight of the cast gone. Mona didn't get it right away, but then recognition spread across her face.

"Oh, you finally got it off, did you? How does it feel?"

It was the way Mona said it, the lightheartedness in her voice, the gentleness of her empathy. Julie could tell she felt bad for her, but she didn't want her pity. Like Dr. Chan, Mona was only trying to be nice. What the hell are they supposed to say? "Sorry your child is still dead" every time they see you?

"Stiff," Julie replied. "It definitely needs physio."

"Well good, I'm glad you're getting back to normal," said Mona, pausing, knowing she had said the wrong thing. "You know with your arm and everything."

Julie nodded, put on the best smile she could muster and said, "Yes, I know what you mean."

A large man in a light blue dress shirt and dark navy tie emerged from a door rubbing his cheek. Ryan followed behind him, listing off some codes for Mona to type dutifully into her computer. Julie thought she looked relieved not to have to talk to her anymore.

"Thanks for squeezing me in, doc," the man said, stepping up to the reception desk.

"No worries, Mr. Hall, you take care and have a safe flight," Ryan said, glancing up. He noticed Julie standing there.

"Sorry, just be a minute," he said, throwing her a smile. The man turned and noticed Julie.

"My apologies for keeping him from you."

"No need to apologize. I'm just happy you got your tooth fixed."

"Pretty, and sweet too," the man said, turning to Mona. "Well ain't he the lucky bastard."

"Yes I am," smiled Ryan, giving Julie a wink.

Julie smiled back, but all she wanted was to get the hell out of there and quit this ridiculous display of normalcy.

Walking to the car, she stopped and stuck out her arms. "Notice anything?"

"Oh, forgot it was today. Hey, let's go out for dinner, what do you say? Celebrate you getting that cast off. When's the last time we went out for dinner, just the two of us?"

"You know when," she said looking at her feet. "Before Kayla was born."

"So, let's go."

"I don't feel up to it."

As they walked to the car, Julie passed Ryan the keys and told him to drive.

In the car Ryan said, "Come on, it will do you good to get out." His voice was so full of positive encouragement that she wanted to smack him.

"A fucking dinner out isn't going to fix anything," she said, turning to face him.

"Well it's better than sitting at home feeling sorry for yourself, now isn't it?" he hissed through clenched teeth.

"And what, then I feel better, and we try having another kid? Is that what you want?"

"I don't blame you for what happened. I don't want you to try and fix this like you do with everything. I just want you to feel better."

"Well, I don't feel better. I won't be feeling better any fucking time soon."

Ryan looked away, rubbing his temple with his hand.

"Jesus Christ, Julie," he said looking at the steering wheel.

"I fucking killed our baby and you want to go out and eat fucking spaghetti?" she said.

"I . . . I . . ." he sputtered.

"I what?"

"I just want it to be normal again," he said, calmly turning to face her again.

"Why have you never gotten angry at me?"

"What do you mean?"

"How can you want to go eat with me when I killed our child? What's fucking wrong with you?" she said. She slapped him on the shoulder with her left hand the way a baby would slap its hand on a tray. He jumped a little, then moved toward his door. She did it again, harder. And again. And again. He let her do it until she grew tired. Then he grabbed her hand.

"It was an accident for Christ's sake. A fucking accident. It was horrible and nothing will change that," he said. He was breathing through his nose, trying to control his temper.

"You're hurting my arm," she said. He let go.

"Sorry," he said, and stared at the steering wheel.

"I don't want to go out. Just take me home, please."

Ryan put the keys into the ignition and drove home.

★

The little girl with the glowing golden hair looked so happy, coming down the aisle wearing a Christmas morning smile.

"We're here, Mommy!" she said to her mother following closely behind.

Julie looked down at her seatbelt and felt fear. She knew they had to get off the plane. She yanked and pulled the buckle but it wouldn't come apart. She was sweating. She pushed the flight attendant button. The mother and the girl were watching her struggle with the belt.

"Can I help you?" asked the mother.

"We have to get off this plane," Julie answered in a voice louder than she intended.

"Pardon me?" the woman said.

"We have to get off this plane. It's going to blow up."

"Pardon me, miss, what seems to be the problem?" asked a flight attendant suddenly appearing by Julie's side.

"I can't get this thing off!"

"She said the plane is going to blow up," the mother reported to the attendant.

"Is that true? Did you say that?" the attendant asked Julie.

"Yes, we're going to die if we don't get off this plane." The seatbelt finally unclipped and Julie stood up.

"Miss, you need to sit back down," said the attendant, leaning down into a small microphone attached to her uniform. "Get me security. We have a possible code blue in row 22."

"Get out of my way," said Julie.

"Miss, I've called security. You just need to sit down and remain calm so we can get this sorted out."

Julie moved around her and said to the mother, "Please, get off the plane. We're going to die."

"Please stop, you're scaring my daughter," the mother said, standing in front of her child, shielding her.

"I . . . I know it sounds crazy, but I know it's going to blow up."

Two male security guards emerged from the front of the plane and marched towards them.

"Miss, can you please come with us?" they asked politely, but Julie wouldn't leave without the mother and the girl. She wouldn't let them die.

The guards grabbed her and she fought them with everything she had. She latched onto the headrest, hugging it as she kicked backwards at the shins of the guards with her heels. She was kicking and screaming as she woke up from her dream, a dream so intense, so real, so visceral, it left an afterimage on her body. The smell of jet fuel remained in her nose, the texture of the headrest fabric lingered on her fingers. Was that a hand mark on her arm? She realized the bed was wet.

"Another nightmare?" Ryan asked, sitting up in bed.

"Yes. I wet the bed, I think," she murmured weakly. Ryan lifted the covers.

"That you did," he said. They got up, and he began pulling off the sheets. Her soggy nightgown stuck to her thighs and buttocks as she walked to the bathroom, shaking. The fabric of her nightie sucked to her clammy skin as she peeled it off and hopped in the shower. The cool water gave her goose bumps, and the memory of the plane washed away as the hot water made its way through the pipes. She increased the temperature and let herself have a good soak. She flexed her hand, stretched it the way the physiotherapist had shown her. It didn't open the way it had before. Two of her knuckles remained enlarged and sore. She closed her eyes and put her head under the hot water. .

The dream had been different this time. They'd never left the ground, and she'd managed to get her belt off. Julie had been thinking a lot about her dreams lately, thought they might have been some sort of Jungian warning about Kayla. Your child is going to die and you need to save her. But now with her child dead, why would she be getting closer to saving her in the dream?

Perhaps a reaction to the loss? Maybe on some level I still think I can save her, she thought. She opened her eyes and squeezed her nipple to see if there was still any milk coming out. Nothing. She squeezed again, harder. Was that a milky drop? Too hard to tell in the shower. The curtain drew back and Ryan stepped in.

"Mind if I join you? You got my leg wet too."

"I'm done," she said as she pulled back the curtain and slipped out of the shower.

"You okay?" She could tell by the way he asked that it was out of genuine concern for her wellbeing rather than an invitation for sex. They hadn't made love since two months before Kayla was born. She had absolutely no desire. None. She felt bad for Ryan. She thought for a second about going back to join him in the shower, but decided against it and opted for a couple of Ativan instead.

"I'm fine," she answered, grabbing the pill bottle from the medicine cabinet. As she was about to close the cupboard door she saw the little bottle of Smirnoff vodka that had resided there since the Caribbean cruise they had taken four years before. The cap unsnapped with a sound like someone had stepped on a tin can, a sound Julie had always enjoyed. She threw the tiny white tablets in her mouth and downed the vodka. It burned and she coughed after she swallowed.

"You okay?" Ryan asked again.

"Just swallowed funny," she answered. She was about to toss the bottle into the trash, but thought better of it. Ryan wouldn't approve of mixing alcohol with medication, but she wanted to sleep without dreaming. To avoid a lecture or an argument, she tucked the bottle between the mattress and boxspring of their freshly made bed. She slipped under the covers naked and closed her eyes, hoping she would fall asleep before Ryan came back to bed.

3

After sweeping up the broken glass, Julie glued the M back onto the framed photo of herself and replaced it on Kayla's shelf. She went to the crib, picked up the stone, kissed it, and gently returned it to its proper place. She stroked the rock as if it were the top of Kayla's head.

I need to run, Julie thought. I need to feel good again. She could fix herself, make it better. The only thing that had ever made it better was running. This would be her first run since the accident.

With determination and focus she double-knotted her shoelaces. Then she stood, ready to go. Reaching for the door handle, she froze. Fear gripped her; her heart began to beat rapidly and pounded so hard it felt like it was coming out of her chest. Was she having a heart attack? Her breath; she couldn't breathe. She pushed herself, grabbed the door, flung it open and stepped onto the porch. The cold air was a slap in the face and Julie inhaled deeply as if she had just emerged from the ocean floor. "I'm okay, I'm okay," she said aloud. She paced around the porch. Once she had calmed down she began to stretch. She placed her left foot on the railing and leaned over her leg, touching her toes. She held it gently, feeling the tightness in her hamstring. She repeated this a few times and then switched legs. Next she pressed up to the wall and performed a sequence of dynamic stretching exercises. When she was done, she walked down the driveway to the sidewalk. "Okay, let's do this," she whispered, and off she went.

It was a cold damp day. Several houses already had their Halloween decorations out and the wind matched their would-be wickedness. Julie felt a chill run down her back and arms, goose-bumping her flesh. Each step forward created the sense of liberation she had been missing. Drawing the crisp air deep into her lungs gave her the feeling that despite all the horror of the past few months, things might somehow turn out okay. She made her way through the Glebe, past the old brick houses recently gutted and refurbished. Their beautiful new facades boasted contemporary light fixtures, mailboxes, and new windows. These were the homes of interlocking brick and organic gardens, espresso machines and a Benz in the drive. Typically they were filled with people Julie didn't much care for; weekend socialists who were only do-gooders because they could afford to be. They were Ryan's clients, and every time she went to the grocery store or the coffee shop she could feel their stares and hear their murmurs: "Look, there's the woman who killed her baby by locking her in the car." Last week she was buying milk when she swore the woman behind her in line whispered, "Baby boiler."

"What did you say?" Julie had asked, angrily spinning around.

"Nothing, I didn't say anything," the woman had said, momentarily pausing the unloading of her shopping basket.

"Oh, I thought you said something . . . *unkind*. Sorry," Julie had said. After she turned back around, she felt the eyes of the cashiers and the people in line staring at her, burning holes into her body. She had paid for the milk and left the store as quickly as possible without looking back.

Her running route took her to the canal and she felt a sense of relief. She was no longer in the proximity of all those judgemental people. Her pace began to hasten joyfully. Why hadn't she started running sooner? This was good; this was exactly what her body and brain needed. Then there it was. The big maple tree, the same one she threw up on the first time she suspected she was pregnant. Bile shot up into her throat and she swallowed hard. Coming towards her was a woman running. She was pushing the same jogging stroller Julie had in the garage. The pain in Julie's stomach grew into a knot and her eyes filled with tears. In an instant the memories flooded back to her. She was back in the woods in the front seat of an RCMP cruiser with a female officer at the wheel. It was dusk when the emergency helicopter had found the car. Julie and Officer Benson were the first to arrive.

"Is that the car?"

Julie nodded slowly.

"You can stay here if you want to," said Officer Benson, opening her door. The police radio chirped and a voice said something Julie didn't understand as she watched the officer run toward the car. Julie opened her door and the smell of grass filled her nose as the heat of the day came roaring at her like a swarm of bees. It was the sound she heard that was the most troubling. Julie didn't understand until that moment that you could *hear* silence. It was an audible thing, silence. There was no car engine running, no cries of a child, and no cries from her aunt. Julie's ears rang with it. Silence.

★

She ran unglued, lost in direction and purpose, her mind awash in guilt and memories. When she stopped she didn't know how far she had run or where she was. She glanced across the emptied basin of the waterway and saw the brown brick monolith of Dunton Tower standing tall at the university. She had covered a good distance for her first run but she didn't feel any of the endorphins that always left her rejuvenated. In fact she had never felt so horribly sad; not in the woods, not even at Kayla's funeral. Looking at the building, she thought about jogging there, making her way to the top and stepping off. It was only a fleeting thought, not one she gave much credence to. She shook her head. It wasn't the option she was looking for. She had a better idea. She began to run again, cutting up to Bronson and then down Glebe Avenue until she reached the liquor store. By the cash at the front of the store she found some single serve bottles of Smirnoff and Absolut Vodka. She grabbed them all. There were several bottles of red wine on the counter, one of which had a label affixed to it stating "Staff Pick." She grabbed one and added to the pile.

"You do know it's far cheaper to buy a big bottle," said the clerk, surveying the collection of miniature bottles.

"They're party favours," she said.

"Oh," he said, "Well I think I have more in the back if you want."

"No, this will be fine, thanks."

Outside, Julie ducked around the corner with her beige paper bag. Her hands were shaking. She snapped the lid off one of the bottles and tilted it all the way back. The liquor burned her mouth and throat. She drank another one. There was a rush of heat in her belly, down her arms and legs; her cheeks flushed pink.

A man walked by in a business suit. His eyes met Julie's. He saw what she was doing and looked away, continuing on. She decided it was time to go home.

Back on her block, she watched a plastic bag dance and spin in the middle of the street, the wind tossing it about in swirling jerks and tugs. It swooped and climbed high into the air, nearly reaching the branches of a massive oak, and then shot back down and scurried across the street. It landed in a yard decorated with fake headstones, skeletons, and a toy crib in which sat a baby. The baby held its green arms up in the air as if it wanted its mother to pick him up. Blood dripped from the child's fangs. It was utterly repulsive, and Julie stood staring, transfixed by it.

"Everyone loves the zombie baby," said a man from a neighbouring driveway dragging a brown leaf bag to the curb.

She turned to the man and said, "It's fucking disgusting."

The man looked taken aback. "It's only in good fun, you know. For Halloween."

"It's sick," she said and walked off.

★

Sitting crosslegged in the middle of Kayla's room, Julie finished another bottle. She tossed it on the floor with all the other empty ones.

She listened. Silence.

4

Her mouth was dry. Her head was a sick accordion that throbbed and wheezed. She went to the bathroom and sucked greedily from the faucet, taking long, noisy gulps. Then she swallowed two Ativan and stepped into the shower once the water was warm. Leaning against the wall and closing her eyes, she allowed the heat to unclog her mind. Gradually she turned the water hotter and hotter, each time letting her body adjust to the temperature until her flesh was pink and the mental fog lifted from her brain. She wrapped herself in a towel, went downstairs and made toast. The coffee that Ryan had left for her was barely lukewarm. She put it in the microwave. In a daze she watched her mug lazily spin counter clockwise behind the glass. Eventually the light inside shut off and the microwave emitted a series of three beeps followed by the higher pitched chirp of a fourth, indicating her beverage was ready. It was the long beep at the end that caught her attention. She opened the door, removed her cup, shut the door and turned it on again for five seconds, listening more intently this time. Beep, beep, beep, bing. It sounded like the bell you would ring when you wanted to summon a flight attendant. She sipped her coffee and did it again. Had it always sounded that way? How was it that she had only noticed now? She did it over and over again while she ate her toast. When she was done, she went upstairs, got dressed and found her car keys. The airport was only fifteen minutes away.

★

On the third level of the parking garage a couple with orange skin and bleached white hair were loading their leopard skin luggage into the back of a black SUV. Julie decided to wait for them instead of endlessly circling in search of a spot. She watched the woman at war with her chewing gum, her long hair pulled back tightly into a braided ponytail. She wore far too much eyeliner, its effects only heightened by the glare she offered Julie for putting pressure on them to move their vehicle. Julie merely smiled and waved to say thanks. A small pink bubble appeared out of the woman's ruby lips, exploding with a pop that echoed through the parking garage. A chill ran down Julie's spine. She was happy to see them drive away.

She stood back near the windows and watched people join the herd slowly twisting through the maze of black poles connected by fabric strips, ready for departure. She sat on a bench and waited. She knew why she had come. She had to see if she could find them before they boarded. She began to grow anxious. But why today? What was it that compelled her to come today specifically? It wasn't the microwave bell. It was more than that. She didn't know what, but she sensed it. Something was telling her to come here, to be watchful.

Her knee bobbed up and down. She held out her left hand, palm down, and clinically observed its shaking. Her heartbeat seemed too quick and she felt the back of her neck moisten with sweat. She wrung her hand, shaking it madly, hoping to somehow calm herself and straighten out whatever damaged nerves were causing this disorder. Pausing, she observed her hand again. Once again it twitched and spasmed. She repeated the procedure and again the tremors appeared. She looked up and saw several people in line watching her. They looked away when she met their gazes. Flustered, she dug wildly around in her purse, groping around until she found her bottle of pills. She tapped out a blue one and swallowed it dry. A woman walked by with her new baby, maybe a month old, slung in a navy wrap around her torso. It was too much to handle. Julie headed to the bar.

"Vodka seven," she said to the bartender.

"We don't start serving until eleven," he said with a smile.

"Oh," she said. "What time is it?"

"You only have ten minutes to go," he said. "Bring it to you then?"

"Sure, that will be fine. I'll just have a glass of water while I wait please."

He placed a glass of water in front of her along with a bowl of pretzels. She thanked him and looked to her right, out the giant window, toward the airfield.

★

The combination of the pills and booze made everything feel unhurried and relaxed. With the world now playing in slow motion, she was able to watch everyone, inspect everyone. Nobody could get by her when they were all moving so leisurely. Every woman and child was scrutinized carefully. Along with the medication and alcohol came clarity, a feeling of reassurance that what she was doing was right and that her actions were somehow in alignment with a greater good she was yet to comprehend.

"It's got to be, right?" she muttered to herself. She heard the sharp high pitched hum, the unmistakable sound of a jet accelerating. Swivelling on her barstool, she watched a plane race along the tarmac, its nose angling away from the earth. A small part of her waited for it to explode, almost wanted it to, and when it didn't, her feeling of purpose began to dwindle. With each plane that left the ground, a small part of her faith went with it. Maybe this wasn't the day? Maybe she shouldn't be here? But then why had she come? Perhaps it wasn't real after all.

"You waiting for a flight?" asked the bartender.

"No," she said.

"A friend then?"

"Yes," she lied. "Coming in from Russia." Russia, she thought. How ridiculous.

"Cool. Can I get you another one?"

"Sure, sounds good."

It was during her fifth cocktail that her cell phone rang. The screen displayed "Ryan Calling."

"Hello," she answered, catching the bartender looking at her. He looked away and returned to polishing glasses.

"Hi. Thought I would check in and see how you're doing," Ryan said.

"I'm good," she said.

"Whatcha doing?"

"Not much, you?" she said, and after she said it she thought it sounded weird. Did she slur?

"I tried calling you at home several times and there was no answer."

"I'm out shopping."

"Shopping?"

"For new running shoes," she said. The bartender glanced at her and then quickly looked away.

"Oh, did you get some?"

"Not yet. Can't find ones I like."

"I'm pretty tired. Why don't I grab some Thai on the way home?"

"Yeah sure, sounds good. See you soon."

"Love you."

"You too," she said, hanging up. She felt her face flush as the bartender continued to polish glasses.

"It's not what you think," she said.

He looked over at her and said, "I don't think anything, ma'am, I just serve drinks. People come in here all the time to meet other people. Sometimes they come off the planes, sometimes they don't. Lots of hotels nearby. I've seen it all."

She didn't say anything. He could think whatever he wanted to. But then she wondered if she should protest, make a stink about it. If she was having an affair, would she be angry at the bartender's comments? He didn't say it meanly, just matter-of-factly.

"I'm only waiting for a friend."

"Moscow flight came in two hours ago," he said. Once again, it wasn't malicious. He wasn't trying to show her up or put her down. He was merely stating, in his own subtle way, that he wasn't a fool.

"I'll just take the bill please," she said politely, a tacit acknowledgement of this fact. As he placed the black billfold in front of her, she saw them out of the corner of her eye. The mother wore a knee-length grey coat and black heels that tapped out a sharp tattoo as she walked. She was holding the hand of a young girl with blonde hair. Julie quickly flipped open the case, checked how much she owed, and tossed down three twenties from her purse.

"Keep the change," she said, getting up quickly.

That had to be them. But now here they were and what could she do? Excuse me but you are about to die? It sounded crazy to her. She would be arrested and they would get on the plane and burn. She hadn't thought this through. Time was running out. They were nearing the security gate. Once they passed through, there was no way Julie could get to them without buying a ticket. Maybe that's what she would have to do?

A piece of paper fell from the woman's purse. Julie ran and picked it up.

"Excuse me," she said.

They kept walking.

"Excuse me," said Julie again, louder this time. It was at that moment she realized what she held in her hand. The woman's boarding pass. The one thing she needed to get through security and on the flight. And now here she was giving it away.

The woman turned and saw Julie waving the boarding pass. The little girl turned around too.

"You dropped this," Julie said, forcing a smile. Not so much over the mistake she had made, but to mask the sensation she was having, a kind of nauseous feeling she had when she went over the top of a Ferris wheel. It wasn't them. Except for the colour of their hair they didn't resemble Julie's dream family in the least.

"Oh goodness me, thank you so much," said the woman, taking the pass from Julie.

"Don't mention it," said Julie, still smiling foolishly. At least that's how she felt. She stood there watching them walk away, disappearing through the security gate. And with them went any sense of purpose she'd had. She was standing in the airport for no good reason. There was no girl. There was no mother. The sensation of being alone, cold, and horribly incorrect gripped her hard, feelings amplified by the towering height of the ceilings and the sheer enormity of the airport. She wanted nothing more than to go home.

She drove, knowing full well she shouldn't be behind the wheel of a car. When she arrived home safely, she found a bottle of red wine and opened it, waiting impatiently for Ryan to return home and for the futility of her life to continue.

★

"Try the sweet chili chicken, it's killer," he said, offering her the silver tinfoil tray.

It was the way he said *killer*. Such a frat boy thing to say. What grown man would use such silly language? It irked her. It wasn't only the word, but how he said it too. So juvenile.

She stared at the meat and asked, "How do you carry on?"

Ryan put the tray down and sighed. He picked up his Chardonnay, took a large swallow and then gently placed the glass on the table. He swirled the yellow wine and watched the liquid spin. Finally he looked up at Julie and said, "I have no idea." He picked up the glass again and drained it back.

"I think you just carry on because you have no other option," he continued, refilling his glass. "I don't know what else to do but carry on."

"I don't mean for this to sound cruel or mean, but it seems easier for you."

Ryan smiled slightly, biting his lower lip. He paused before saying, "Maybe so. Maybe I make it look easy, but every day I stitch myself together out of the broken pieces I find. So I carry on, yes, but I walk with a limp no one can see. I thought you could see it, for a time at least, but apparently I'm a better actor than I thought."

He picked up the wine and swirled it again.

"I'm sorry."

"Don't be. It's not something we can change and it's not your fault. I've never blamed you and I never will. I should have come with you. It's as much my fault as yours or your aunt's or anyone else's for that matter. Was it your aunt's fault she had memory problems? No. Shitty things just happen sometimes and there's nothing you can do about it. We carry on because there is nothing else we can do."

Julie didn't say anything. She looked at him. The lines in his face and forehead looked deeper. He looked tired. He had been keeping the show going while she took the time to fall apart. It was yet another reason she loved him.

Finally she said, "Thank you for keeping everything together. You don't have to carry all the weight alone."

"You carry enough for both of us, and then some."

"I'm still having the dream."

"Want to talk about it?"

"No, not really. It's only . . ."

"What?"

"It's more real than ever. It's like I'm really there."

"Tragedy can heighten the senses."

"Maybe so," she said, letting it go. He was tired and she couldn't bear the thought of sucking any more energy from him by starting an argument or by giving him something else to carry. Besides, Ryan was a man of science and cold hard facts. Dreams and visions didn't fit well into his world paradigm. This she knew she had to keep to herself.

She reached for the chicken, scooped a little onto her plate adjacent to the snowball of rice. She took a bite.

"Killer chicken," she said.

5

Opening her eyes she saw Ryan standing above her holding a pill bottle in one hand and a vodka bottle in the other.

"I've told you how dangerous this is. You can't be doing this, Julie." His voice held the resonance of a concerned parent. His face emanated disappointment.

"I'm not a fucking child," she said, turning over and taking the duvet with her, huddling into a ball.

"You're supposed to be going back to work tomorrow."

She didn't say anything. It was a death sentence that had been coming for a while. The thought of all those sympathetic eyes on her, everyone walking on eggshells, not wanting to upset her, it was too much to bear. How could she face those people? She couldn't even stand going to the corner store, dreading she might run into someone she knew.

"I don't think you are even close to being ready," Ryan said. He stood there waiting for her to react, to say something. She didn't. She only wanted him to leave.

"Julie, I'm talking to you," he said, and paused again. The silences between his words were growing louder, unbearable. She hated those sounds. Why wouldn't he just leave her be?

"I want you to see Dr. Chan again or that Dr. Bell fellow he recommended. You need to get an extension on your leave," he said.

Silence.

"Julie, I'm talking to you," he said.

"What the fuck do you want?" she yelled, sitting up. "You're not even grieving the loss of our daughter! What the fuck is wrong with you?"

Ryan remained quiet and still. His arms hung by his sides; he looked like he was waiting to catch a bus. "I'll call your work for you and tell them you're going to be off a few months more and that I'll bring them a doctor's note."

"I'm never going back there!" she screamed.

"Fine, quit, whatever, we don't need the money. I do however want you to call Dr. Chan or Dr. Bell and make an appointment. I've taken all the pills away. If you need a pill, you can ask me for it."

"Bastard," she said.

"Julie, I only want you to get better. All this medication and booze is not going to help you."

"Why aren't you sad? Why aren't you fucking sad? Are you a goddamn robot or what?"

"I am sad. I'm fucking horribly sad and I'm doing the best that I can."

"Well I guess I'm not doing so fucking well now am I?" she cried, the tears pouring down her face. She was sick of crying, sick of feeling this way. What she had said wasn't fair and she knew it, but she couldn't help herself. She couldn't stop her rage. It was as if someone else were taking over and she was merely watching herself say and do things she normally wouldn't have dreamed of doing.

"Please, promise me you'll call the doctor."

She sighed, reaching for a tissue from the nightstand. "Fine."

"Thank you."

She reached out with both arms. He came to the edge of the bed and bent down and wrapped his arms around her. Julie dropped her hand and began to undo the belt of his pants.

"Hey, what are you doing? I've got to get to work."

"Fuck me," she said.

"Let's do this later," he said, standing up. "When you're feeling better."

She didn't let go. Working quickly, slapping his hands away, she undid the belt, button and zipper, and then yanked his pants down. He looked displeased.

"Jesus Christ, Julie," he said, pulling up his pants. She rubbed the fabric of his underwear, stroking him. He stood still, holding his pants, then finally let go as her hand reached under the elastic band of his briefs. She felt him grow hard as she stroked him.

"Make me feel good," she whispered, leaning in. "I just want to feel good for a change. It's been so long . . ."

"Okay," he said.

She ground herself against him, focusing on nothing but her own pleasure. When she finished, a multitude of new emotions exploded inside her. She rolled off Ryan and sobbed uncontrollably, almost hysterically. He stroked her hair and shushed her, but she was inconsolable. Eventually he got up and put his pants back on. Then he tapped four tablets of Ativan onto the nightstand.

"Two for this morning and two for the afternoon. I've got a very busy day, but I'll see if Doug can take a few patients so I can leave a bit early. I really want you to call that doctor."

Julie nodded, only doing so because she wanted him to leave. When he finally did, she grabbed all four pills off the nightstand, stumbled to the bathroom and swallowed them down with a short suck from the tap. Then she lay back down, closed her eyes, and fell asleep.

★

She awoke as she usually did these days, screaming. The smell of burning hair and jet fuel haunted her and clung to her nose. Breathing heavily, the smells dissipated after a few minutes. The clock read 1:45. She felt numb. Her mind empty, her motivation to do anything was nonexistent. There were no desires, no cravings. She wasn't hungry and she felt nothing except her body resting on the mattress. Eventually she realized her mouth was dry. She sat up and swung her feet to the floor. She didn't get up right away. Instead she instinctively reached for a bottle of pills.

"Fuck," she said.

In the bathroom she discovered the medicine cabinet had also been cleared out. She drank some water from the tap and then got dressed. She found her purse and car keys and moved quietly out the door. She heard the sounds of insects, that high pitched hum. She felt that all too familiar knot in her stomach when she thought about Kayla in the car and about how she must have suffered. She put on her sunglasses. The temperature had risen and it was an exceptionally hot October day. Record-breaking, according to the radio. She switched it off as she made her way south on Bank Street to the large LCBO near Walkley Road, away from the Glebe and Ottawa South, in an attempt not to be recognized,. There she bought a dozen mini bottles of vodka and a screw-top bottle of Chilean red. She paid in cash so Ryan wouldn't see the transaction on the credit card bill.

The car was warm when she got in. She was about to crack the window when she decided to leave it. Now it was time to find a place to drink.

6

The South Keys Shopping Centre parking lot wasn't very busy. She parked near the Loblaws, leaving three empty spots between herself and the last car. Reaching into the paper bag, her fingers found the top of a bottle. Twist, snap, drink. She tossed the empty onto the floor of the passenger's seat. She reached back into the bag. Twist, snap, drink. After the fourth bottle she opened the wine, pouring it into an empty Tim Horton's cup sitting in the cup holder. It was getting very warm in the car. The dashboard indicator told Julie it was 25°c outside and 38°c inside the car. She popped the glove box and snaked her hand down to the bottom. It came up with a pill bottle she had stashed. Three blue pills were all that remained. They slid down the plastic cylinder and into her mouth where they were smoothly washed away with Merlot.

Julie began to feel lightheaded, dizzy. She let her mind drift to it now. She imagined the heat in the car, hotter than this car. The indicator now read 40°c. She twisted the key in the ignition, firing up the engine. Cranking the temperature gauge to the top of the red, she threw the heat to maximum. This is how hot it would have been. Dehydration. Twist, snap, drink. She chased it down with more wine.

Her mind swirled with images: her reflection in the window of her aunt's car, a rock in her hand; the face of the little girl on the plane, her flesh bubbling into blisters; her aunt's body carried through that grassy field on a stretcher; Ryan crying at the funeral; her father in his coffin, her mother in hers. Twist, snap, drink. The gauge read 44°c. Sweat rolled off Julie's nose and dripped into the wine. The ripples from the drops of perspiration seemed to flow in slow motion. In fact everything was slowing down. She turned on the stereo and managed to find Miles Davis' "Autumn

Leaves." Her eyes grew tired and she closed them. She drank the wine while listening to the music and imagined herself running through the woods. Yes, this time she would make it, this time she would get there. She was running without effort, soaring through the woods, the trees golden and lovely. Yes, she knew this time she would make it. It was going to be okay, she could even take her time and look around. Such a hot day, and the leaves, they were big lazy flakes afloat in the air. Golden honey and red licorice leaves fell about her. Wasn't it grand? It was so beautiful, so wonderful. So warm for autumn leaves. What was she supposed to be doing anyway? Oh yes, Kayla, in the car. And where was it? There, up ahead, right where she left it, still running. She picked up a rock and smashed it against the window. It went through without difficulty, and she could feel the cool air emanating from inside the car. A mosquito was biting her arm and she slapped at it.

"Can you hear me? Can you open your eyes and tell me your name?"

Julie opened her eyes. There was a man standing over her, a paramedic by the look of his uniform. He was saying something, asking her a question.

"Can you tell me how many pills you took?"

She was lying down, moving away from her car. She could see her car door open, the window smashed out, popcorn pieces of glass littering the parking lot. A crowd of shoppers watched with horrified faces. What were they all looking at? She turned her head and there on the other side was another group of people staring at her. Why were they all looking at her? She tried to sit up but the strap across her chest restrained her. She looked at the crowd of people again. Maybe they could help her? In the middle of them stood the young girl with the bright yellow hair, the hands of her mother resting on her shoulders. Julie's eyes widened and she tried again to sit up. The belt across her chest didn't move.

"I need to . . ." she said, pulling at the oxygen mask covering her face.

"Leave that on," said the paramedic, pushing her hand away. He repeated his question about the quantity of medication she had consumed.

"I need to save her," Julie said as she was loaded into the back of the ambulance.

"Save who?" asked the paramedic.

"Please, I need to speak to that woman," she said weakly.

"You need to just lie here and stay with me. How many of these pills did you take?" he asked again, holding up the bottle.

As the ambulance pulled away, Julie looked out of the rear windows trying to catch another glimpse of the girl with the blonde hair. There she was. And she was looking at her. Julie felt as if the little girl could see right through the tinted glass. But it was only a flash and then the girl was gone. Julie fought as hard as she could to get up, screaming that she needed to save her. She fought until her vision went black.

PART 3
VISIONS

I

Julie pulled the blanket tightly around her, managing to wrap it over her head so that only her face was exposed. The woman in the next bed was breathing softly, her inhalations rising up to the cusp of a snore and then tumbling down into a sputtering series of wheezes. The window curtain was open a foot and through it Julie watched the storm outside. Large sections of the overcast sky lit up randomly, followed by thunder crackling long and low. Julie had always enjoyed thunderstorms, but she didn't feel good about this one. She thought about Ryan. She should call him, but then remembered the phone was off-limits at this time of night. I'll call him first thing in the morning, she thought.

Way off in the darkness a lightning strike illuminated a solitary plane. Julie bolted up, the blanket still wrapped around her. Her heart began to race as she rubbed her eyes and strained her ears listening for the high pitched sound of plane engines failing. Nothing. No explosions, no fire, only flashes, snapshots of the plane making its perilous way to the airport.

Pulling at the blanket, she let it fall around her onto the bed. She felt exhausted, empty. She only remembered feeling like this once before, shortly after her mother had died. She called it her Humpty Dumpty feeling. It was the sensation of walking into public places and interacting with people as if she were only a shell, a fragile hollow egg made up of cheap jigsaw puzzle pieces held precariously together. If someone was to push her over she would shatter into thousands of pieces and nobody would ever be able to put her back together again. She had no energy to do anything but sleep, yet sleep was the last thing on earth she wanted. She couldn't face another round of the little dream girl on fire. Not after Kayla and after all she had been through. Julie hated hearing the little girl's screams, which had recently metamorphosed into Kayla's screams from the car. These shrieks echoed in Julie's head whenever she took a shower, so now she only showered once a week. The medication she had been given left her mouth dry and made everything taste foreign. She took a sip of water from the bottle on her nightstand. It tasted synthetic. Her toes found the edges of her slippers and she slid her feet into them as she stood up. She put on a bathrobe and wandered down the hall. An orderly mopped the floor around the nurse's station where a nurse read *Fifty Shades of Grey*. She put the book down when she saw Julie approaching.

"Can't sleep, honey?"

"No, not really. Thought I'd try the TV, that usually knocks me out."

"I can get you a pill if you want?"

"No, I'm okay, thanks."

"Must be the storm. Lil is in there trying the same thing."

The door to the common room was closed but Julie could see Lil's profile through the large adjacent window. Julie had spoken to her a few times over the last few days. She thought Lil looked like the Girl with the Dragon Tattoo. Multiple silver studs ran along the flesh of each ear, and more decorated her eyebrows, nose and lower lip. The flesh of her arms was tattooed in thick, black gothic swirls. Crisscrossed razor scars ran up and down her right forearm, while the left was wrapped in a white bandage. Her knees were held tight to her chest. She didn't look at Julie when she came in, but remained focused on whatever she was watching. Julie sat down at the other end of the long couch.

"It's fucking scary shit," Lil said without turning her head.

Julie looked at the TV. The burned, scarred face of Freddy Krueger stared back from behind his iconic bladed glove. It struck Julie as somewhat odd that they allowed psychiatric patients to watch such violent films. But then everything these days seemed odd.

Julie watched despite her desire to get up and leave. She didn't dare suggest they watch something else because Lil frightened her more than the movie did. Julie half expected Lil to suddenly jump up and bite her or worse, slash her own wrists in front of her. Julie found the film compelling, watching the teenagers pop caffeine pills to stay awake so they wouldn't become Freddy's dream food. She could relate.

"You're the lady who locked her kid in the car, aren't you?" asked Lil, snapping Julie out of her trance. She didn't feel rage and she didn't feel sadness. She thought Lil's question should have provoked one or the other or both, but it didn't. It did nothing. Julie felt nothing. She was Humpty Dumpty, and only a shove away from a great fall. Maybe Lil would give her that shove tonight.

"Yeah, that's me," said Julie, intentionally keeping her eyes on the screen.

"That sucks," said Lil. She didn't say it meanly, only matter-of-factly.

"Yes, it does."

"Sorry."

"Yeah, me too."

They watched in silence some more. When a commercial came on, Julie asked, "So why are you in here? Crazy like the rest of us?"

"You want the long or the short?"

"Up to you."

"Fine," sighed Lil, "I'll give you the long, since I dig your face, but I'll make it short. My stepfather started raping me when I was eight. After a series of delightful foster homes, I began engaging in the world's oldest profession at fourteen, banging ass-holes for money to feed my habit. I've been in and out of rehab, juvie, and mental institutions for years."

"Just because you have sex for money, it doesn't make you crazy. What happened to your arm?"

Lil looked thoughtfully at her bandage and Julie wondered if she was making up a story to tell her.

"I'm what they call a cutter," said Lil, holding up her other arm so that Julie could get a better look.

"Why do you do that?"

"Negative attention. I thought it was cool. Sometimes I do it out of old habit. But I don't really do it anymore."

"Is that what happened to your arm?"

"Sort of, but not really. I got this shitty job working in this restaurant. I was doing dishes and prep, cutting radishes for their fucking garden salads. The kitchen staff were always goofing around. The one line cook, Gary, I think he had a thing for me. Anyway, I was cutting the radishes and the next thing I know Gary had slipped handcuffs on me. He cuffed me to the cutting board. I don't even know why they thought it was funny, because what's funny about that, right? So I'm like 'Ha ha, very funny, now give me the keys.' Well everyone went about their business, ignoring me, snickering. It had gone on too long and I was getting pissed. So I picked up the knife and said, 'You think this is funny?' and I cut my wrist with the knife."

A shiver went up Julie's back as Lil made a slashing motion, re-enacting the scene.

"The problem was this," said Lil continuing, "I did it again when I didn't get the reaction I wanted. I went deeper than I intended. It was a real mess. Needless to say, good old Gary never got laid."

Julie laughed despite herself. There was something very intense about Lil, and Julie could vividly imagine the scenario. Did Lil just make that up? Maybe she was a pathological liar? Perhaps that was why she was in here. Julie believed her though. She had no reason not to. The movie came back on and they went back to watching as if they'd only just exchanged small talk about the storm outside or something equally trivial.

At the next commercial Julie expected Lil to ask her why she was here, but instead Lil eloquently said, "Got to take a piss," and left. Julie closed her eyes. Suddenly she felt very tired. She let her body relax into the couch. She closed her eyes. This is nice, she thought.

She awoke to the sound of a baby crying. She was alone. Lil wasn't back yet. Someone had turned off the TV. Was it Lil? And there it was again, the cry of a child. Julie got up, opened the door and stepped into the hall. There was no sign of the orderly who had previously been mopping. The odour of disinfectant filled her nose and made her eyes water. She listened and, sure enough, there it was again, a muffled wail. It was coming from down the hall.

"Kayla?"

The cries grew louder as her slippers flapped against the linoleum.

"Kayla, are you there?"

The nurse's station was empty except for the paperback that had been left open face down. "Hello?" Julie called out. She was answered with another cry. Down the hall she crept until she reached the broom closet. The cries were coming from behind it.

"Anyone in there?" she asked.

It was with a sense of dread that she reached out to turn the knob. Her hand shook. It was locked. The cries grew louder, turning to high-pitched shrieking. Julie pulled and twisted with both hands. "Help me! Somebody, help me please! There's a child stuck in here!" she yelled over her shoulder. And then to the door she whispered, "It's okay, baby. Mommy's coming."

She turned her head again, continuing to yell for help. Julie jumped back and let go of the door handle. Standing before her in the middle of the hallway was the little girl from her dreams, her once soft flesh now burned and scarred. Her blonde hair was singed to her scalp and Julie could smell the horrible sickly odour of seared flesh and scorched hair. The girl opened her mouth and Julie expected her to scream, so much so she covered her ears with her hands. No sound came. A red spot formed on the girl's lower lip. Julie watched it fall, waiting for it to splatter on the tile floor. But when it hit, it didn't. Instead it bounced and rolled, coming to rest against Julie's slipper. She looked at the girl again, and this time a green spot formed on her lip. It fell from her mouth and went bouncing across the floor. They were candies. Skittles. One after another they appeared and fell. Within seconds a colourful water-fall of candies flowed from the child's mouth and danced audibly about the floor. Julie stepped back and slipped on the candy. She crashed to the floor, awash in a wave of brightly coloured sweets intent on carrying her down the hallway. Her arms were moving, trying to keep her atop the candy. She was swimming in the current, watching the little girl grow smaller as she was carried away.

Somebody had her by the shoulders, shaking her. Julie opened her eyes.

"Hey, wake up, you're going to miss the end of the movie," said Lil, removing her hand from her shoulder. It was the vividness of the dream, not so much the imagery, which frightened her. As always, the smells of her dream lingered. Burnt hair and the contrasting smell of Skittles battled for dominance, swirling apparitions in her sinuses.

"Hey, you okay? Freddy visit you in your dream?" asked Lil.

"Something worse."

"Yeah, cool," said Lil, returning to the television.

"Think I'll go to bed, I'm pretty beat."

"Suit yourself. I'm going to watch these bitches die."

Feeling exhausted and weak, Julie shuffled over to the nurse's desk.

"Can I have something to sleep?"

"Sure," said the nurse.

"Can you just give out medication like that? I mean, doesn't the doctor have to sign off on it?"

"Dr. Pratt has it listed on your file. 'As required,'" the nurse read off her clipboard.

"What is it?" Julie asked as the nurse handed her a small blue pill and a paper cup of water.

"Just a very mild sedative."

She tossed back the pill and chased it down with the water.

"Thanks."

"You're welcome. Get some rest."

Julie took a sip of water. It tasted of iron. She sipped again and put the glass back on the little side table. The taste, as if she had been chewing on tinfoil, lingered. Her tongue roamed the back of her teeth looking for relief, but it made no difference. She continued.

"I remember the feeling of the sand squishing between my toes as I ran out of the water. I remember turning around, ready to gloat, ready to call him names. The water, it was as flat as glass. I mean, that's how I remember it: flat as glass. It probably wasn't that flat, but that's how I remember it," she said, running her hand along the brass buttons fastening the brown leather to the dark lacquered wood of the chaise longue on which she lay. She looked past Dr. Pratt and studied the framed degrees and certificates cluttering the wall behind him. She looked down at her legs, at her blue running pants. Ryan had been so kind to bring them, along with her other clothes, toiletries and MP3 player. He would be coming to see her after this session was over. She stroked the fabric of her thigh and thought about how lucky she was to have him.

"How old were you when it happened?"

"I was eight. Luke was ten," she answered, glancing at the doctor. "And you know what the most haunting image is for me? It's not my father diving and screaming in the water, or even the police pulling his body from the water, it's my brother's unfinished book sitting split open, spine up, on the arm of his chair waiting for him to come back and finish it. It's that image which haunts me, that open book on the arm of that chair."

Dr. Pratt sat back, pushing his glasses back up the bridge of his long nose. He took in a breath and quickly blew it out. "That's a lot to carry."

A tear fell from Julie's right eye.

"Do you blame yourself?" he asked.

She nodded.

"That's a big burden to carry around for thirty years," he stated calmly.

She nodded again, wiping her eyes. Dr. Pratt held out a box of tissues.

"I'm sorry," she said, taking one.

"Don't be," he replied, pausing, waiting for Julie to finish blowing her nose before she continued.

"I mean, yes, I blame myself, but I understand it wasn't my fault. I didn't push him into the water. I didn't hold his head down. I should have never asked him to go into the water though. He wasn't a good swimmer. So why did I want to rub that in his face?"

"Maybe because you were an eight-year-old girl who wanted to prove that she was good enough to her older brother, good enough to hang out with him and his friends? Is that a possibility?"

"Maybe," she said, turning away, looking back at her knees.

"What was your parents' reaction? Do you think they blamed you?"

"They told me it wasn't my fault, but I never believed them, well at least not my dad. I mean, he told me over and over, especially when he was drinking, that it wasn't my fault. The thing was, it always seemed artificial, as if he was trying to convince himself that it wasn't my fault."

"And do you think what happened to Kayla was your fault?"

"Absolutely," she said, turning back to him. She felt her face flush as a wave of anger engulfed her. She tried to remain calm by focusing on her breathing.

"Why do you think it's your fault?"

"Because I let my baby die of fucking heat exhaustion in the goddamn woods! I mean, Christ, she didn't get there by herself. I put her in there. *I* put her in that car."

"Is that what you were doing in the parking lot? Were you being Kayla?"

Julie didn't answer. Dr. Pratt made a note in his book. Her nostrils flared like the wings of an insect as she lay back down on the couch and gazed up at the ceiling.

"Are you still having your recurring dreams?" asked Dr. Pratt, the tone in his voice remaining smooth, calm.

She didn't want to answer.

"No," she muttered meekly.

Dr. Pratt wrote something down on his pad. It made her nervous when he wrote, as if somehow everything were going to be brought forward in some Kafkaesque trial that would be happening in the near future. All her failings and all the flaws in her personality would be exposed and she would be found guilty of being a deficient human being.

"That doesn't sound very convincing."

"Fine. I'm still having the dreams," she said with modest exasperation. "And what the fuck are you writing down in that little pad of yours?"

"Why did you lie?"

"Because you don't believe me."

"I believe you when you tell me you're having nightmares."

"Not that. You know what I mean."

"Yes, I know what you mean," he said, placing the pad and pen on his lap. "I'll tell you what else I believe. I believe you may have seen a mother and a little girl standing in the crowd the day you were pulled from a car with heat exhaustion and a belly full of wine and pills. The little girl may even have had golden hair. However, do I think they are the people from your dream? No, I don't. Memory is a tricky thing, Julie. People see what they want to see and remember what they want to remember."

"So, what? You think I'm making all this up?"

"Not at all. Again, I believe you when you tell me you're having recurring dreams."

"And you think they're caused by feelings of guilt over Luke?"

Dr. Pratt's eyebrows rose. "Is that what you think they're caused by?"

She was losing her patience for Dr. Pratt's doublespeak, answering questions with questions.

"If there's something wrong with me, if I really am crazy, then it's your job to fix me."

"Yes, I'm here to help you. Crazy is a very broad term. Do you consider yourself to be crazy?"

"No."

"Good. Neither do I."

"Then what's wrong with me?"

"Do you think your dreams are caused by the guilt you hold over your brother's death?"

She looked up at the ceiling and thought about the doctor's question. Could it be? Was this some sort of manifestation of her remorse?

"Maybe," she answered eventually. "Ever see *The Eyes of Laura Mars*?"

"Pardon me?"

"*The Eyes of Laura Mars*. It's a movie with Faye Dunaway."

"No, I haven't. What's it about?"

"It's about a woman who has recurring visions of a killer."

"So you think you're having *visions*."

It was the way he said it. *Visions*. Maybe he didn't mean to say it the way she felt he'd said it, as if she was crazy after all. Perhaps she had said too much? Perhaps she should keep her mouth shut if she ever wanted to get out of this place.

"I know what you're going to say."

"Your precognition seems to be growing stronger by the minute," he said with a smirk.

It was the perfect thing to say. It diffused the tension in the room and made her laugh. It was why Dr. Pratt was likeable, why she trusted him.

"Not what I meant. You're going to tell me that many people dream about planes crashing, but it doesn't mean they're having visions. And I understand, given the millions of people in the world, somebody will have a dream about a plane crash, and sure enough one of them will be right, based on nothing more than coincidence and statistical odds."

"I wasn't going to say exactly that, however something close. So why do you think your dreams are more real, more special?"

"I never said I did."

"The Eyes of . . ." Dr. Pratt paused, trying to remember the title.

"Laura Mars," Julie said, and the doctor wrote on his pad of paper. Julie assumed he was writing the title.

"Yes, you said it was about a woman who has visions. Why did you bring that up?"

"Because what if they are real? I mean, maybe I'm supposed to save them?"

Dr. Pratt wrote something down.

"I know what you're going to say," she blurted before he could ask her another question.

"My job as a therapist is becoming easier and easier. I wish all my patients knew what I was going to say, then I could just stay home."

Julie smiled. "I think you're going to tell me I have these dreams because I want to save Luke and Kayla."

Dr. Pratt's eyebrows again ascended into the flesh of his forehead. He nodded but didn't say anything. Julie felt he was waiting, pausing, acknowledging this moment in her therapy where a breakthrough of some kind, major or minor, was taking place. She nodded back.

"That could be it," she lied.

"Yes, I think so. I'm glad you came to it on your own," said Dr. Pratt, writing again on his pad of paper. "Why don't we call it a day and talk again tomorrow?"

"Sounds good," said Julie, sitting upright and placing her feet on the floor.

"Ryan coming to see you?"

"Should be waiting for me."

"See you tomorrow then."

"Think I can go home soon?"

"It's been seven weeks. You've put on some weight and you're eating again. I think we've made a lot of progress so yes, I think you can go home soon. Maybe for Christmas."

"Thank you, Dr. Pratt."

He smiled and told her she was welcome.

3

They could see their breath in the plummeting afternoon sun. Ryan held her hand as they walked along the path through the park beside Island Park Drive. Blotches of snow sat in the crevasses of intersecting tree branches and clung to the bright green grass in patches. Julie didn't say anything. She reveled in the sensation she was experiencing, a fragile exuberance, the kind of sensation she had after a long run or after she orgasmed but without the climatic high of either. It was a sensation normally reserved for high school kids falling in love on a first date. It had been such a long time since they had just held hands, when there had been no consoling, no tears, and no second guessing of feelings. Maybe this was this fresh beginning she was hoping for? Could they start over? Maybe have another child? No, too soon to think about that. Just enjoy this moment, she told herself.

"Dr. Pratt thinks I've been having these dreams because of what happened to my brother and Kayla."

Ryan turned to her. He looked tired. He'd been waiting to hear this, she could tell. She didn't elaborate, waiting for him to agree with Dr. Pratt's assessment. Instead he turned his head back and looked straight ahead, then down at his shoes. He was thinking about what she had said. As they continued to walk, her feeling of exuberance began to evaporate. Maybe he didn't agree? Or maybe he believed she really saw the woman and child from her dreams?

"What do *you* think?" he asked without looking at her. She heard a thin tone of skepticism in his voice which told her she better nail this or she might wind up spending Christmas alone at the nuthouse.

"I think he's absolutely right. I think it was the stress of work and training for the race and feelings I never really dealt with before, about my brother. That's why I began to have the dreams, and after what happened to Kayla I think I melted down with guilt. I wanted someone to save, wanted to fix the mistakes I made so much that I believed these dreams were true. I know now they were accidents. I know that. I can never really forgive myself though, you know?"

Ryan nodded. "You need to forgive yourself, or you can't move on."

"I can't, Ryan, I just can't. I can accept they were accidents, and I can live with that, but I can never ever forgive myself for what happened. No matter how much therapy, no matter how many pills I take, forgiveness is not an option."

"I forgive you. I love you. I want you to come home now so we can be together again."

When he said those words "I forgive you. I love you," a dam of emotion released inside her, splashing down her neck and arms, down her spine and legs and out her fingers and toes. Ryan wrapped his arms around her and held her tight. She shuddered and wailed in his arms. She kissed him hard on the mouth and told him she loved him, told him she was sorry.

It was then she began to doubt her own beliefs for the first time. There had always been doubts, but this time it was different. As cliché as it sounded to her, it really was a like a light switch had been turned on inside her head. A Gestalt paradigm switch. Could the things she was saying actually be the truth? Were these dreams really only complicated manifestations of her feelings of guilt? Was she really mentally ill? Yes. She had been sick. Sick in her mind. And with this revelation, outside in the winter air, there came a sensation of liberation. Liberation and acceptance. She was crazy and had been so for many months, if not years. Not schizophrenic crazy, not bipolar crazy, but crazy nonetheless, and that was crazy enough. The acceptance of this fact was freedom. An epiphany.

After she had calmed down, they strolled back towards the hospital, hand in hand. For the first time in a very long time, Julie wasn't sad.

4

The snow was falling in giant flakes, and when Julie opened the passenger door and stepped out into the wind it was like she had stepped into a freshly shaken snow globe. The cold air stung her eyes and they watered ever so slightly.

"You okay?" asked Ryan, retrieving her bag from the back seat.

"Really happy to be home is all," she said, smiling.

Inside, the house was warm and smelled of pine. Ryan had bought a Christmas tree. He had decorated it with white lights and red ribbons and placed it in the corner of the living room next to the gas fireplace, above which hung a silver banner. "Welcome Home!" it read. She stared at the sign, noticing the creases in its surface where it had been folded in its packaging. Imperfect. Something Ryan likely picked up at the dollar-store. She understood why he had placed it there. It was his kindness, his thoughtfulness, his love. However, it was a pin prick. So small as to be almost insignificant. But there it was nonetheless, a reminder that she had been away. Welcome home—a pin prick. She could feel the air coming out of her mental life raft. She had been away. The sign reminded her of *why* she had been away. It was a dunce cap. A pink triangle. A red X. Looking at it made her feel ashamed. She knew this wasn't Ryan's intention, but all she wanted to do was run over and rip it down. The house was so clean, and the tree and the fire looked so perfect, and there was the sign reminding her why it was this way. There was no baby to mess it up, no toys to clean, no dirty dishes in the sink left there due to exhaustion. It was back to the home of two people with no kids.

"Looks really beautiful, Ryan," she managed to say.

"Are you hungry, I went and got . . ."

She spun and kissed him hard. She felt his surprise, or was it resistance? She pulled back and looked at his face. He smiled. She kissed him again and this time felt him relax and let go. She rubbed the crotch of his jeans and felt the stiffness there. Tugging at the buckle of his belt, still furiously kissing, they staggered backwards until they fell onto the couch. They removed each other's clothes quickly and before she knew it he had slipped inside her, thrusting with powerful strokes.

"What about protection?" he said, stopping suddenly.

"It's okay," she said. "Come inside me."

"Are you sure?"

"Yes. Now shut up and keep going."

When he shuddered inside her, she wrapped her legs tightly around the underside of his buttocks and pulled him into her. She held onto his hips as he collapsed on top of her.

"Welcome home," he panted.

She closed her eyes and thought maybe, just maybe, this was going to work after all.

5

There were people everywhere. It made Julie anxious. She hadn't been out in a crowded public area since her uncle's funeral; even that was small in comparison. She had never had issues with open spaces before, rather the opposite. Planes and elevators made her uncomfortable, but now she felt her heartbeat racing. People were looking at her. They knew what she had done, knew that she had let her baby die and had been locked up at the nuthouse because she couldn't cope with it. No, no, no. She knew this wasn't true, and had gone over it numerous times with Dr. Pratt. She knew it was only a thought in her head. They had even practiced going out in public together. The truth was nobody knew who she was or what she had done. This fact made her smile. She had a grip. She was better. Sane, in other words.

Julie switched spots with Ryan, sitting down and sharing the wooden bench with a family of three kids. It was the first weekend the Rideau Canal was open to the skating public and it was extremely busy. The temperature had risen to -2C and the sun was blazing in a cloudless sky. Julie loosened the laces and wrenched on the tongue of her skate, pulling it forward as much as she could to make room for her foot. She tried pushing her foot into the skate, but it wouldn't quite go. She yanked at the laces some more and pulled again on the tongue. This time her foot slid in easily. She repeated the process with her left skate, even failing to open it wide enough the first time. Ryan helped her up.

"Feel good?" he asked.

"I haven't been on skates in three years, maybe longer."

"You're an athlete, a natural."

"You're the skater, not me. Skiing I can do. This? Not so much," she said, stumbling forward holding on to Ryan's hand for balance. They glided rather ungracefully, away from the hive of skaters and the swarms of people lined up to purchase Beavertails and hot chocolates from the stands set up along the edge of the frozen waterway. The crowd thinned and Julie's sense of unease faded with it. She took in a big breath of cold winter air and let it out.

"You okay?" he asked.

"Just getting my balance," she replied, not disclosing her true feelings because she *wanted* things to be normal. She didn't want him to look at her with his hospital face. It was the face he would sometimes wear to the hospital when he came for visits; a kind of worried concern combined with pity and sadness. It was an expression people pulled out for funerals or trips to the old folks' home. She didn't like it. On one visit she had told Ryan he looked constipated and this had made him laugh. He had promised to lighten up. But then there were the visits where she couldn't get out of bed and his hospital face would return with a vengeance. She didn't want to see it out here in this sunshine, in all this splendour. She wanted to be normal, wanted to be sane again and she was determined to show Ryan she was that person. By pretending to be that person, she knew she would become that person again. She didn't know if she actually believed it, but she *wanted* to believe it. Routine. Repetition. Do normal things over and over and eventually you become a normal person, right? Take it easy. Give it time, Julie, she told herself, repeating the advice of her doctors, repeating the advice of her friends, repeating Ryan's advice. Take it easy. Give it time.

A teenaged boy ahead skidded to a stop, playfully spraying his girlfriend with a wave of ice pellets. The girl batted the air laughing and squealing. It was the sound of the skates, the crunching sound that took Julie's mind back to the car and to the rock sliding down its side. It wasn't even a similar sound, but something about it, perhaps the speed of it, took her back there. The image of the rock rolling down the side of the car replayed itself over and over in her mind's eye. She skated on, holding Ryan's hand, smiling, pretending to be happy. Then she saw herself running with the rock, like she was watching a movie in her head. She watched herself fail again and again as they continued to skate towards Parliament Hill. Even though she replayed it, it began to fade. Her brain was beating her with the image over and over and by doing so rendering it powerless. You can only watch for so long before the image loses its power, she thought. Feelings of grief and guilt subsided; mind monsters slowly sank back into their cerebral swamp.

As they coasted to a stop by the National Arts Centre, Ryan asked her if she would like a hot chocolate. She told him coffee and asked if he would line up by himself because the crowd was freaking her out a bit. He said no problem, and she watched him skate away. No problem, no concern in his voice, no hospital face. He was sweet.

She stood in the middle of the canal and watched people whiz by. The skate had done her good. Exercise had always been her thing. They hadn't gone far enough or worked hard enough to get the kind of high she felt at the end of a long run, but this was a good start, definitely better than lying in a hospital bed doped up. She took a deep breath in through her nose and exhaled through her mouth, repeating this a few times until she felt better. However, as she stood there, watching everyone swirl about her, her sense of wellbeing slowly dissipated, replaced instead by a sense of unease. Look at all these people, she thought, a hive of bees, coming and going in plentiful hoards, full of purpose and goals. Who are they? Where were they going with such conviction? How can they all be so *happy*? The thoughts immobilized her, paralyzed her, made her feel inhuman and a stranger. It was an odd sensation for her because she'd never experienced anything close to it before. This wasn't the feeling of not belonging at a party or some other social scene, but something deeper. It had a physicality to it. Could this be an anxiety attack?

"Here you go," said Ryan, reappearing at her side.

"Boy, you were fast," she said, taking the coffee.

"Yeah? Didn't feel fast," he said. "Beavertail?"

Julie grabbed one of the cinnamon and sugar coated pastries. "Thanks, baby."

She was trying desperately to put on the façade of normalcy.

"Are you okay? You seem a little shaky."

"Fine," she lied. Ryan was sporting his hospital face. "I'm fine, really," she repeated.

"Okay," he said, his expression morphing back to cheerful. It was then, out of the corner of her eye, she saw them skate by, the girl and her mother.

Julie dropped her coffee.

Ryan looked in the direction she was staring. Then he turned back to her. "What? What is it? What's wrong?"

It was there, in that moment, that everything depended on what Julie did next. Years of dreaming, years of anxiety, years of anger and frustration and fear leading to her stay in the hospital. Could she let them just skate away? Could she just let it go? She could see these questions on Ryan's face. If she went after them, would he forgive her?

"I'm sorry, but I'm not crazy," she said, passing him her food. He grabbed at her as she spun around and skated away.

"What? What are you talking about?" he yelled after her.

In ten quick glides, Julie had caught up to the woman and her child. She could see the blonde hair of the girl sticking out of her grey sock monkey toque. What to say? How does one begin this conversation? "Excuse me, but I've been dreaming about you for years."?

Julie skated behind them for a while, her thoughts racing through her head, not knowing what to do. A pink scarf fell out of the woman's backpack and landed on the ice, allowing Julie the opportunity to pick it up and yell at the woman, "Excuse me, you dropped this."

The woman and child continued to skate away. Julie repeated herself louder. This time the woman stopped and turned around. Julie held up the scarf so the woman could see it. They glided towards each other.

"Oh thank you," said the woman.

"You're welcome," Julie said, trying to smile. It wasn't them.

She had made the same mistake again. She'd only seen them for a second out of the corner of her eye, but she'd been so sure.

"What the hell, Julie?" asked Ryan as he skidded to a stop beside her. "What was that all about? Who were they?" He turned his head and looked at the woman and the girl skating away. When he turned back he didn't have to say anything. He knew.

"You thought it was them?"

Julie nodded as she began to cry. "I want to go home," she said meekly. "I just want you to take me home, alright?"

6

The snow was falling outside the window. Across the street Julie watched as two young children and their father rolled up big balls of snow for the body and head of a snowman. Ryan had gone to work, grumbling about having to perform a double root canal on Mrs. Rosewood, a consistently rude patient with horrendous halitosis. Before he left he'd kissed Julie on the forehead and reminded her of her appointment with Dr. Pratt at 11:00.

It was almost 10. Julie thought about what she was going to say. The image of the woman turning around with the wrong face, the face of a stranger, kept grating at her. How could she have been so wrong? A mistake. Another mistake, like leaving Kayla in the car. No way to fix it. Maybe this is what she would talk about. Her need to fix things, her need to make things right. Maybe he could help her let go of that part of herself, teach her the acceptance of the way things were. Then again, why change who you are? If you don't like yourself, that's why. She was no longer part of the Julie fan club.

In the bathroom she looked at the pill bottles with her name on them. She looked at her face in the mirror. Tired. Haggard. She uncapped a bottle and let a pill fall into her palm, then repeated it with a second and third bottle. Cupping her hand, she tossed all three capsules into her mouth. She rolled them around her tongue like candies. Then, instead of bending down and sipping out of the tap, she spat the medication into the toilet. The pills bunched together at the bottom of the bowl and Julie flushed.

The snow was letting up, the sky lightening, blue ozone and sunshine about to find its way through. I'll run to the hospital, she thought, it will do me good. By the time she had changed into her winter running clothes, strapped on her rubber cleats, and locked the front door behind her, the man across the street was screwing a large carrot into the face of his snowman.

The air stung her face and burned her lungs and Julie relished it. Running in the cold air made her feel alive. It grounded her and gave her a sense of calm. The only issue with running in the snow was that it was easy to slip and pull something or roll your ankle. An inch of wet sticky snow lay atop the sidewalk and her feet were quickly soaked. She jogged onto the side of the slushy road streaked with tire tracks and the footprints of pedestrians who'd given up the unplowed sidewalk. She caught the green light at Bank Street and picked up her pace. When she reached Bronson, the sidewalk had been both cleared and salted. She shortened her stride down the hill, treading carefully to avoid a slip. She felt her hamstring muscles tighten on the descent. Once the ground leveled out she picked up her pace again. It had been months since she had run. Hell, it had been months since she had done anything more than lie in bed and cry. Now look at me running, she thought. This is what she needed more than anything, to run. Running was her medication—not pills in little bottles. Her mind grew quiet. She focused on her breathing, relaxing her arms and her posture. She sprinted by the brown brick Civic Hospital where Kayla had been born to the adjacent Royal Ottawa Hospital. She slowed to catch her breath, and pulled her phone from her pouch to check the time. Twenty-five minutes. She looked up and caught her reflection in a mirror window. She looked thin. She thought about Ryan holding her hand when she was lying on her back giving birth to Kayla in the hospital, the hospital she'd just sprinted past. Ryan's face, telling her repeatedly that she was doing great and she was almost there. Twenty five minutes—who gives a shit. Why had she checked her time? Habit? Maybe. She moved closer to the mirror and inspected her lined face.

"Stupid, dumb, selfish cunt," she whispered to herself.

"Did you run here?" asked Dr. Pratt, coming around from behind his desk.

"Yes," said Julie, plunking herself down in the patient chair.

"Well that's good now isn't it?"

"Not really," she said sullenly.

"Why, don't care for the snow? You're dressed for it."

Julie didn't answer. Instead she kept her head down and scratched at the armrest of the chair.

"How's your week been?"

"Fine."

Dr. Pratt came and sat down across from her and said, "Doesn't sound so fine." Julie looked up at him.

"I went skating with Ryan on the canal and I thought I saw them, the woman and the little girl."

"Tell me about it," he said, placing his notebook and pen neatly on his lap. She told him about her feelings of isolation as she stood on the ice and watched the people skate by. She told him how she debated whether to go after them. She told him everything and he listened without interruption, only occasionally jotting a quick note down on his pad. When she was finished her story she punctuated it with, "So am I still crazy or what?"

"Listen, just because you thought you saw people from your dream, *again*, it doesn't make you crazy."

"So says the psychiatrist," Julie spat.

"You want to be crazy, fine. You want me to up your medication, fine, we can do that too. But quite frankly, I don't think you do. You seem to be very in touch with your own feelings and very self aware. I think you have been through a lot of trauma in your life and you haven't forgiven yourself yet. What do you think? Do you think that's an unreasonable statement?"

"I just want to stop having nightmares of the little girl and her mother burning to death on an airplane. That's all I want."

"How did you feel when the lady on the canal turned around and you realized it wasn't her?"

"Disappointed. Confused. Maybe even a bit angry."

"Why did you feel disappointment?"

"Because it wasn't them," answered Julie in a tone that implied this was an obvious fact.

"Why disappointment though rather than, say, relief?"

"Because I want them to be real?" said Julie, unsure if she was asking a question or giving an answer.

"Here's the thing. You can't, or rather, you shouldn't be feeling disappointment for people who are imaginary unless you don't think they're imaginary."

"Come again."

"I'm saying, in our previous sessions, you came to the conclusion that these dream people were really only manifestations of your own guilt and nothing more. For example, when a child wakes up on Christmas morning and comes downstairs and doesn't find presents from Santa, the child is disappointed, firstly because there is nothing to open, but also because Santa has let her down. This kind of disappointment requires a belief system, a belief system which regards Santa as real. If I go downstairs and see no presents, I'm only disappointed with my wife."

This made Julie smile. "You don't believe in Santa Claus?" she asked.

"Only the mall kind. What do you believe, Julie? Do you believe the dreams you're having are real?"

"No, of course not. Maybe disappointment was the wrong word? Then again, no, it wasn't the *wrong* word. It's like when the woman turned around and it wasn't her, I was disappointed because I thought, finally, here is a possible explanation for what is happening to me other than just some manifestation of guilt. I mean, why do I dream about the same people over and over and over again? And they always look the same. These aren't people I've ever met and not even composites of people I know. How do you explain that?"

Dr. Pratt leaned back in his chair and adjusted the glasses on his face. "The brain is capable of the most wonderful creations. Think of those patients with multiple personalities, they have whole groups of fully formed people living inside them—not that I'm in any way implying you suffer from such a disorder. However, to dream the same people over and over is, in my opinion, nothing extraordinary. In fact, I might even say it's common. Often people will dream of an imaginary place or person their entire life. Nothing wrong or bizarre about it. In your case, I think you've had unresolved feelings about your brother's death since you were a child. I believe these feelings were manifesting themselves prior to the accidental death of your daughter, at which point these feelings of guilt and remorse were compounded exponentially. In other words, you were pushed over the edge emotionally. And who can blame you? I'm actually surprised at your resilience. Most people don't make as quick a recovery as you have. Then again, you're still having your dreams, aren't you?"

Julie nodded.

"When's the last time you dreamt about them?"

"Last night."

"I can't promise to make the dreams go away, but together I think we can continue to chip away at why they keep occurring. Maybe then they will drift away."

"Maybe," Julie lied.

"How's Ryan?"

"Fine. Supportive, as always."

"Good. Supportive is good. I like Ryan."

"I feel I'm still letting him down. I mean, how do you kill someone's child and expect to move forward together?"

"Listen, how many times have I told you, you didn't kill anyone and Kayla was your child too. I know you. If there was something else you could have done you would have done it, correct?"

"Yes of course."

"If roles were reversed, would you have forgiven him?"

Julie thought about it. "I don't know," she answered, continuing to puzzle over the question. She envisioned Ryan trying to smash the window with the rock. He could have done it.

Dr. Pratt didn't say anything.

"I mean, I guess I would," she said at length.

"Do you think he has forgiven you?"

"I know he has."

"How do you know?"

"He told me so. Told me he still loves me."

"That Ryan, I like him more and more. Do you believe him?"

"Of course I do."

Dr. Pratt made a note on his pad. Whenever he added to his notes Julie grew somewhat uneasy. "Why is that?" he asked.

"Why shouldn't I? I can tell. He isn't a good liar."

"If Ryan can forgive you, why can't you forgive yourself? If you don't, well then I don't think your dreams—dreams deeply rooted in guilt—will leave you."

"I'm not there yet," she said, staring down at the floor.

"That's okay, we're going to work on it, together," said Dr. Pratt.

Julie looked up and offered a small smile. Maybe she could forgive herself in time? She supposed acknowledging this possibility was itself the conceivable beginning of forgiving herself.

"Maybe I can," she said.

When she left Dr. Pratt's office, Julie felt a sense of optimism she hadn't felt in a very long time. She also felt drained physically and emotionally. Maybe she should take the bus home? In the lobby, heading for the main front door, someone called her name. Turning around she saw Lil clad entirely in black. If it weren't for the studded dog collar, green hair, and all the facial piercings, Lil, with her white as snow face and rouge circles staining her cheeks, would have looked like a porcelain doll.

"Yo, bitch, where you going?" Lil asked as she raised her right hand alongside her head. Julie realized Lil was coming in for a high-five. She went with it and they slapped palms midair. It was a juvenile gesture that made Julie smile, but coming from Lil it felt honest. Genuine.

"I'm day-passing girl. Whatcha doing here, want to grab a coffee?" Lil asked. Julie's first reaction was to say no. When she left the hospital she never thought she would see Lil again, let alone go for coffee. But they had spent a good deal of time talking after the night they met in the common room. Lil was little more than half Julie's age, but a smart kid nonetheless. Mature beyond her years in fact. Julie had developed a soft spot for Lil. There was just something about her.

"Sure, let's grab a coffee."

7

They sat in the coffee shop and Julie listened as Lil went off on a funny rant about Randy, a bipolar patient who believed the mashed potatoes were haunted by the spirit of Humphrey Bogart. About twenty minutes after Randy ate them in the hospital cafeteria he would inevitably recite the dialogue from *The Treasure of the Sierra Madre*.

"So I tell him," says Lil, laughing so hard she was barely able to get her story out, "I tell him that the Jell-O contains the spirit of Elvis. Well bloody Randy loves his Jell-O, yeah, and now I've fucked it up for him. He looks terrified, but grabs the bowl and wolfs it down in two seconds as if it was some horrible tasting medicine. I swear to God, ten minutes later he's belting out *Are You Lonesome Tonight*. It was friggin unbelievable. What a fucking voice the guy has! We need to put him in a talent show. Tomorrow I'm going to tell him the scrambled eggs contain the soul of Doris Day and see what happens."

This got Julie laughing pretty hard.

"So, you still dreaming your dream family or what?" Lil asked.

"Yeah," answered Julie, sipping her coffee.

"Dr. Pratt still telling you it's a manifestation of repressed guilt?"

"Yeah," Julie answered. She was surprised how crude Lil could be and then suddenly so articulate.

"I think that's bullshit," said Lil, waving her hands in the air.

"Why's that?"

"Because ghosts, souls, the afterlife, aliens, precognition, telepathy, the lost city of Atlantis, you name it, I believe in all that shit."

"Bigfoot?"

"Okay, Bigfoot is bullshit, but the rest is for real. For *real* real. You hear me?"

"I hear you," said Julie, "I just don't believe you. I mean, I believe you believe, I just don't believe in all that ESP UFO *shit*, as you call it."

"Why not? I mean come on, man, you're the one having the crazy dreams. I've never had dreams *close* to that. I don't know anyone who's had dreams like that. I'm telling you, this isn't some repressed bullshit. What you're having is for real."

"Then what does it mean?"

"Fuck if I know."

"Well that's really fucking helpful now isn't it?" said Julie, finishing her coffee.

"Hey, don't get pissed at me, I'm on your side. I believe you. I believe *in* you. I think the people you dream about are real."

"Now you sound fucking crazy."

"I'm on a day-pass from a mental hospital," said Lil, grinning.

"So what am I to do, assuming you're right, assuming that these people are real. What am I to do? I'm sick of dreaming about them. I'm losing my mind because of them. What would you do?"

"You told me when you came to in the parking lot, as they were loading you into the ambulance, that you saw them."

"Yes."

"Well fuck, there you go," said Lil. Julie didn't have a clue what she was saying.

"I don't follow."

"You go back to the parking lot and case the joint."

"Case the joint?"

"Yeah. You sit around and wait until they show up again."

Julie arched an eyebrow. "You want me to sit around the parking lot where I almost killed myself and wait for an imaginary family to show up?"

Lil leaned forward, put her hand atop Julie's and said, "They're not imaginary." A shiver shot up Julie's arm like she had been stung by a wasp. Lil continued to stare at her.

"I'm serious, Julie, and you know in your heart I'm right. Trust your feelings on this."

"How do you know I'm not just crazy like Randy?"

"I never said Randy was crazy," said Lil. Julie was puzzled until a big smirk washed across her face. She leaned back in her chair. "Randy's a goddamn loon," she laughed.

"I don't know. Even if you're right, what makes you think I'll see them in the parking lot again?"

"I don't know about you, but I get my groceries from the closest store, and I do so over and over. She'll be back."

Julie paused and said, "Thanks for the coffee."

"Let's swap numbers," Lil said, pulling her cell phone from her pocket. Julie reluctantly exchanged numbers thinking Lil would be the last person she would ever call. She liked her, but Lil was just a kid. Still, there was something charming and intense about her which make Julie like her.

They hugged goodbye outside the mall and Lil made Julie promise to visit when she got released.

8

It was five days before Christmas and the store was packed. "Can I help you find something?" asked a young woman at Julie's side. She wore her thin brown hair in a ponytail, and her nametag read Amber.

"How much are they?" Julie asked, pointing to the green binoculars in the glass display case.

"Those ones are fifty-five. What are you using them for?"

"Birding," answered Julie. Amber's question made her nervous.

"Not a lot of birds this time of the year," Amber said.

"Christmas gift," said Julie with a smile.

"Nice gift."

"I'll take 'em."

Ryan had gotten up early and made egg white omelettes with tomatoes, feta, and fresh basil. He had cut a pink grapefruit in half for them to share, sectioned it and even took the time to slice the bottom so it wouldn't wobble on her plate. He'd laid out rye toast, orange juice, and coffee.

"Wow, this looks great," Julie said, sitting down.

"Hey, you seem to be in a good mood," Ryan said, looking up from the newspaper.

"Yeah, I slept well for a change. No nightmares. And boy that coffee smells great. In fact everything smells great." Julie had made the difficult decision to stop taking her medication two days ago, and since then her olfactory sense seemed to have made a comeback. The metallic taste which had constantly lingered in her mouth was gone. She didn't feel dopey. The fog had lifted. But she hadn't told Ryan or Dr. Pratt yet. She wanted to see how she felt first. If the nightmares got worse or she felt suicidal in any way she vowed to get back on them. It was only the beginning of day three, but she felt a hundred times better. So far, so good.

Picking up her coffee, she brought it to her nose and breathed in the earthy aroma. "Wonderful," she said.

"Can I take the car or do you need it?" he asked.

"Can I drop you off? I was thinking of going to see Sally." Sally was Julie's close friend. She had visited Julie twice in the hospital. After Sally had her second kid, she moved out to Kanata. Going way out to Kanata was a perfect excuse for Julie to keep the car.

"Yeah, sure, great. I'm happy to see you're getting out to see a friend."

Halfway down a row of cars she lucked into finding a strategic spot near the entrance. She flicked on her indicator and waited for the older woman in the dark blue Plymouth to vacate the spot. Five days before Christmas and the lot at South Keys was packed. The Loblaws was a hive of people coming and going, their carts piled high with hams, turkeys, and all the trimmings. Julie watched in awe at the flow of shoppers. After the first hour, Julie grew bored and decided to make a game out of it. She'd brought a pen and a pad of paper with her. She didn't know why; she figured she should have one on a stakeout. Stakeout, she thought. How ridiculous that sounded. What the hell am I doing here? What a waste of time. Lil, the gothic seventeen-year-old foster kid, had planted this seed. Now she was sitting in a parking lot watching Christmas shoppers while waiting around for her dream family to show up. Better than drinking and popping pills, though, she thought. Then again, maybe not.

It was crazy. She'd lied to Ryan about needing the car to visit Sally, but she couldn't shake the feeling that what she was doing was right. Sitting there made her feel excited, like she was doing something important. Crucial even. She could suddenly understand how someone could strap explosives to their chest and blow themselves up. It was more than belief in a cause, it was the experience of something divine, holy, and pure. It was knowledge in something outside the realm of the every day. Maybe it was precognition, maybe it was something from God, but whatever it was Julie knew in her heart it was right.

Grabbing her coffee and taking a sip, she spied a middleaged mother wrestling with three kids climbing all over her shopping cart. She was yelling at them and trying to pull them off as she continued into the store. Julie jotted down their description and the time they went in. She repeated this for other patrons: Overweight man in jeans and black leather jacket: 10:15. Mother, daughter, both blonde, matching pink jackets: 10:16. Father with two kids, boy, girl: 10:17. In ten minutes she had a full page of people, and she decided to track them to see how long they shopped. The first one she recognized was the overweight man, emerging at precisely 10:34 with a case of Diet Coke.

She played this game all afternoon, only leaving her post once to use the in-store bathroom. People generally took about forty minutes to complete their shopping. One woman, though, took over two hours. Julie thought she had missed her while she was in the bathroom. What could she have been doing? Who knows. Sitting in the car wasn't so bad. The game she had created kept her mind occupied and the time passed surprisingly quickly.

It was slightly past 3:00PM when, three rows of cars over, she saw a woman walking alongside a young girl with blonde hair. She grabbed the binoculars off the passenger's seat and brought them to her eyes. Blurred images of cars swirled before her. It was disorienting. "Fuck, where are you?" she asked, lowering the lenses to locate them. There, she found them, and raising the binoculars again she spun the centre wheel with her index finger. Their faces came gradually into focus. It wasn't them. She cursed and tossed the binoculars onto the passenger seat. She rubbed her face and groaned. The exuberant feelings about being here for a reason were beginning to wilt. Maybe this isn't right? Why do I always doubt my instincts about this? Maybe I should just take my medication.

As the hour approached 5:00, Julie turned the ignition key and started the car. It was time to pick Ryan up from work. She pulled out of the parking lot, still keeping her eye out for them as she drove away.

A few minutes later, she pulled into Ryan's parking lot to find him waiting for her

"How was Sally?" he asked.

"She was busy today, so we're going to try again tomorrow."

"Oh, that's too bad. What did you get up to then?"

"Cooking shows," she shrugged.

"Oh. Do you have a surprise dinner waiting for us at home?"

"Actually I thought we could go out to eat."

When they came home from dinner Ryan threw on some Miles Davis and plunked down on the couch. "Would you like a glass of wine?" Julie asked, wanting a drink herself.

Ryan frowned. "Do you think it's a good idea to drink while you're on your medication?"

"One glass won't hurt, will it?"

Ryan poured two glasses, and they drank them in front of the fire. They both talked, but managed to tiptoe around anything to do with Julie's state of mind, the possibility of another child, or the hospital. Julie was happy about that. She was tired of talking about her feelings. It was boring and unproductive. The wine was making her feel relaxed.

"I love you so much," she said, and she meant it.

"I love you too," said Ryan, smiling. Once again Julie thought about all his positive qualities, and felt lucky to have him in her life. When they finished the bottle she suggested they go to bed.

Julie awoke in her dream. She was in her seat in the airplane. The woman across the aisle was smiling at her. "Good sleep?" she asked.

Julie rubbed the armrest with her hand. This was real. This *is* real. "Funny," she said. "I had the funniest dream. Actually, not so much funny as real. I don't mean real as in really *real*, but it felt so real. It was like I was there."

"What was your dream about?"

"I was living with this man and it was almost Christmas and we were sleeping together."

"Now we're talking, sister," said the woman laughing. Julie felt herself blush. She looked around the plane and thought to herself, How can this be a dream? This *must* be real.

And then came the explosion.

Julie woke up screaming, clawing the air. Ryan grabbed her and pinned her arms to her chest, telling her repeatedly that it was only a dream.

When she'd calmed down enough, he allowed her to go to the bathroom where her medication bottles sat waiting on the counter. She picked them up and rattled them so that he would hear, but didn't take any. She only drank some water from the tap before reluctantly returning to bed.

After dropping Ryan off at his office, she repeated the previous day's surveillance. Woman in ugly flowered hat: 9:15. Woman who spent too much time in tanning bed: 9:16. Family of four, mother in black hijab: 9:17. Gay man in white sunglasses: 9:18.

By 10:30 she had to go to the bathroom, and grabbing her cell and purse headed reluctantly inside. Rounding her car she bumped into a woman carrying several bags of groceries.

"I'm so sorry," Julie said.

"Not to worry," said the woman as a little blonde girl stepped out from behind her.

PART 4
SAVING HER

When Julie turned around and saw her brother was gone, she would never have described what she felt as a *feeling*. It was far too overwhelming, devastating, and shocking to be tagged, classified, and placed into a singular emotional box. But whatever set of powerful emotions were running through her back then were running through her again now.

"Are you okay?" asked the woman. Julie was staring at the little girl. For several seconds she didn't know if she was dreaming or awake.

"Are you okay?" the woman asked again.

"Yes, sorry. I'm a little out of it today. All this Christmas running around I suppose," Julie managed.

The woman smiled. "I know what you mean."

Julie's mind was racing. How to engage this woman in conversation? How had she missed them going into the store? Should she let them go and then follow them? She needed something, and needed it immediately.

"You know, you look really familiar to me," was what came out of her mouth.

"Oh," replied the woman and her puzzled expression remained, thankfully, quite friendly. "I'm not sure. You also look vaguely familiar. We shop here a lot, don't we baby?" The young girl simply nodded. I look familiar, thought Julie, because you saw me get taken away in an ambulance.

"Do you work around here or something?" Julie asked.

"Um, no," said the woman. Julie could tell this was going to end quickly. The woman didn't want to answer any more questions; she wanted to get moving and put her bags down.

"Maybe the gym?" Julie blurted.

"Mommy goes there all the time. She likes to work out."

Julie chuckled. "Which one?" she asked, but the woman didn't seem forthcoming. The girl answered instead.

"She likes to go to the YMCA."

"That's where I know you from, the YMCA. I'm Julie," she said to the woman.

"I'm Lindsay, and this here is Margo."

"Well it was nice to *bump* into you. If I see you at the gym I'll say hi," Julie said, trying desperately to keep herself composed.

"You too. Come on, Margo, we have to get going."

"Here, let me help you," said Julie, taking a bag from Lindsay's arm.

"Oh that's not necessary," Lindsay said, but she let her take the bag anyway. Julie followed them to their vehicle, a black Pathfinder, and she immediately made note of the licence plate number. Lindsay thanked her, and she replied that it was the least she could do.

After they drove away, Julie scrambled back to her car and wrote down the licence number. Then she walked into the grocery store and made straight for the bathroom. Emerging from the stall, she noticed her hands had begun to shake. Her knees felt weak. She managed to make it to the counter before she buckled and collapsed to the floor. She leaned forward and pulled her knees to her chest. The trembling subsided after a few minutes but her body felt boneless, and for a moment she thought she might be sick. Slowly she managed to pull herself up and splash water on her face. It played in her head over and over—*they're real, they're real, they're real*. Walking in a daze to her car, her eyes filled with water and she began to cry in loud, fractured sobs. After several minutes she regained her composure enough to open her car door and get inside. She placed the key in the ignition and turned.

"Let's go," she said aloud.

2

After she'd filled out all the paperwork and paid for a trial month at the YMCA, Julie agreed to the offered tour. In the lobby she took a seat on a bench and called Sally. Maybe she would see her after all and tie up that loose end. She felt guilty about lying to Ryan, and if she saw Sally it technically wasn't a lie anymore. The last thing she wanted was for Ryan to find out she'd been deceitful. Besides, she needed to talk to someone about what was going on, and who better than her oldest and dearest friend. Sally would know what to do next.

"Hello?" answered Sally's frazzled voice. Julie could hear her boys screaming and laughing in the background.

"Hi, Sally, it's me."

"Julie, oh my God, I was just thinking about calling you. I love when that happens. It's like I'm psychic or something. Does that ever happen to you? You know, there you are thinking about someone you haven't seen in a long time and bam, there they are. Weird eh?"

"Yeah, really weird."

"Are you out of the hospital?"

"Got out last week."

"Oh that's great. How are you feeling?"

"Much better now."

"Good, good. Well it would be great to see you some time."

"What are you doing now?"

"Just a sec," said Sally. Julie listened as she pulled the phone away from her ear to scream at her sons. "Sorry about that. They're driving me nuts today. What were you saying?"

"I asked what you were doing now."

"Well, right now I'm making the boys grilled cheese sandwiches, which seems to be the only thing they'll eat."

"Do you want some company?"

"Ah, listen, I need a break. Rich is here, he can watch the boys. Why don't I meet you for coffee?"

The way she said it, though, Julie could tell she didn't want her to come over. Was it because she'd been in the mental hospital and Sally didn't want crazy around her kids? She was godmother to Sally's oldest for crying out loud. But never mind, she was happy to be seeing her friend.

They made arrangements to meet an hour later at the coffee shop in the Glebe they'd been going to for years. After she hung up, Julie noticed her hand was shaking again. She waved it in the air like it had fallen asleep. "Get it together," she whispered to herself. She looked up and across the lobby where a homeless man sat. He had a thick grey mustache and beard with nicotine stains in the corners of his mouth. He was staring at her. His eyes were wide and in that way, and several others, he resembled her companions at the mental hospital. He stood up, carrying several plastic bags in each hand. Julie leaned back as he came to a stop in front of her.

"I see things too," he said.

Julie said nothing.

"I know you see them too," he went on, and Julie leaned further back.

"I don't know what you're talking about," Julie said, standing up and scooting around him, heading for the doors.

The man yelled after her, "You can't change the future!" and Julie froze. She turned and glared at him. He stood there staring back. Finally she turned away, and pushed outside into the cold winter air.

3

Sally hugged Julie when they met outside the coffee shop. "So good to see you," she said. "My God, Julie, you're shaking. What's wrong?"

"Do you mind if we go get something stronger than coffee?"

"Sure, sure. Let's go."

They walked down Bank Street to the Royal Oak. The bar was fairly empty but Julie selected a table tucked away in the farthest corner. It was dark inside and it made Julie feel more at ease.

"What can I get you ladies to start?" asked the waiter, placing two menus on their table.

"I'll take a double bourbon on the rocks and a pint of Guinness," said Julie. The waiter's eyebrows lifted in surprise.

"Just a coffee for me," said Sally.

"I was just going to brew a fresh pot, shouldn't be too long. JD okay? Closest we got to bourbon."

"Yes, that's fine," Julie answered. When the waiter left Sally gave her friend a look of disbelief.

"What are you doing, Julie?"

"I just need something to calm my nerves."

Sally frowned. "Should you be drinking? Aren't you on medication?"

"I stopped taking it."

"Why?"

"I didn't feel good on it. Everything tasted horrible."

"What happened, why are you so upset?"

"I saw them."

"Saw who?"

"My dream family. I mean, I didn't just see them, I ran into them, literally bumped into them in a parking lot."

Sally's brow wrinkled in puzzlement. "I don't understand."

"The mother and the little blonde girl from my dreams, they're real."

"They're real?" repeated Sally sceptically.

"Yes, really real."

"And you just happened to run into them in a parking lot?"

"Sort of."

"What do you mean, sort of?"

"When I . . ." Julie paused to collect her words, "I saw them first as I was being loaded into the ambulance when I almost killed myself in the parking lot—which was an accident, for the record. For a while I thought I'd just imagined them, that they weren't real, but my dreams have kept right on going and now they're so intense and so real I have problems distinguishing when I'm dreaming and when I'm awake."

"So you went back to the parking lot to, what, see if you could run into them again?"

"Yes."

"So you have been staking out the parking lot at South Keys?"

"Yes," said Julie, pausing as the waiter returned with the drinks.

"Did you ladies have a chance to look at the menu or are you just here for drinks?"

"Just drinks," said Sally, passing him the menus.

"Alright then, just yell if you need anything else," he said and left. Sally watched as Julie picked up the Jack Daniels and drained it back in one go. The ice rattled in the glass as Julie placed it back down. She felt the booze burn down her throat, felt the heat of the alcohol shoot down her arms. She took in a big breath and blew it out. Then came a sense of calm.

"Feel better?" Sally asked. She was looking at Julie with a hospital face exactly like Ryan's.

"Yeah. Listen, I'm okay," Julie said, leaning forward and lowering her voice to almost a whisper. "I know what you must be thinking. She's off her meds, drinking again, and now she's seeing imaginary people."

"Not exactly. Well maybe," Sally said.

"They're not imaginary. They're real. I've been dreaming about them for over four years now and they're real. Real as you and I."

Sally covered her mouth with her hand.

"What is it? What's wrong?" Julie asked. Sally seemed to be on the verge of tears.

"Sweetie, I think you're still sick. I think you need to get more help. Maybe we should call Ryan?"

"Sally, Sally, listen to me. I'm not sick. Remember when I called and you said you were just thinking about me and then the phone rang. Remember that?"

Sally nodded.

"Well I don't think it's just coincidence. I think on some level we all have some sort of ESP. You thought of me and the phone rang and it was me. You said it yourself: you love when that happens. This is the same thing. Well not the same, but similar. Listen, Sally, I've been dreaming the same nightmare for four years. I know these people like my own family. You have to trust me when I tell you this is them. You believe me, don't you?"

Sally shrugged. Julie knew how crazy it sounded. Maybe telling Sally was a bad idea. What if she phoned Ryan? Julie had to convince her but didn't know how.

"Listen, Julie, have you ever thought that maybe you just saw a couple of people who looked similar to the people in your dream?" suggested Sally.

"No. I mean, of course I have. It's actually happened before. I thought I saw them the other day skating down the canal, but it wasn't them because I know what they look like," Julie said. Sally didn't respond. "I *know* what they look like, Sally."

Again Sally sat silently staring at her friend. Julie could tell she wasn't buying it. "What does Ryan think?"

"I haven't told him yet. He's at work. I wanted to talk to you first. I don't think he'll believe me, and now I realize you don't either."

"Listen, sweetie, I think you saw people who might look like the people in your dream, but they can't be." Sally said. "It's just not possible."

"How about if it were? How about *The Mothman Prophecies*?"

"The movie with Richard Gere?"

"Yes, good, you know it."

"Julie, sweetie, that's a movie. It's not real."

"But what if it was? What happens if that movie, which is based on a true story, is real?"

"So is *Girl Interrupted*, so is *Sybil*."

Julie leaned back in her chair and wondered if there was any way she could turn this around. "I'm not crazy," she said. "I may be having dreams or visions or whatever you want to call them, but I know in my heart this is real."

"Okay, let's say these people are the people from your dream. What do you want me to do?"

Julie reached into her pocket and slid a piece of paper across the table.

"What's this?" Sally asked.

"Does Rich's brother still work for the police?"

"Yeah."

"It's their licence plate number. I want him to run it and find out her last name and where she lives."

"Julie," said Sally, shaking her head, "this can't be done. Peter could lose his job if he got caught doing something like that. And even if he could, and even if he did, what would you do? Would you go up to them and say, 'Hi, I'm Julie and I've been dreaming about you for four years. Oh yeah, and by the way, you're both going to die in a horrible plane crash.'"

"I don't know," said Julie. She understood Sally's point because she didn't know what she would say herself. Julie pinched at her lower lip as she thought about it. "I don't know," she repeated.

"Maybe you should talk to Ryan about this."

"Will you ask Peter for me? You could explain it to him. He's always thought you were cute, right? You even told me once when you were drunk you thought he might have a thing for you."

"Jesus, Julie."

Julie leaned across the table and grabbed Sally's hands like they were about to pray together. "Sally, please, I need your help on this one."

"I can't."

"Please. If you can't do it for me, do it for Lindsay and Margo."

Sally recoiled slightly. "Those are their names, Lindsay and Margo?"

Julie nodded. She could feel Sally wanting to let go, but she kept a firm grip on her hands.

"Fine."

"You'll do it?" asked Julie, still holding on tight.

Sally looked Julie straight in the eye and said, "Yes, I'll do it. Promise." Julie released her grip and Sally leaned back in her chair.

"Oh Jesus, thanks so much," Julie said, taking a sip of beer. The alcohol was going straight to her head. She felt lightheaded but calm. Still, the thought that Sally might tell Ryan kept presenting itself. What could she do? If Sally told him, Julie would just have to deal with it.

"What are you going to do now?" Sally asked.

"I'm not sure," Julie lied.

4

"How was your visit with Sally?" asked Ryan, fastening his seatbelt.

"Good," answered Julie. "She actually came to see me and we went for a drink at the Oak."

"Not coffee?"

"She said she wanted a glass of wine."

"Three boys, don't blame her."

Julie smiled and nodded. Ryan looked at her like he felt something was off. "Are you okay?" he asked.

"Fine, why?" She was doing her best to act normal. Perhaps she should tell him, get it over with. Then again, if she did, she might find herself back in the hospital. A little time was needed first to ensure everything was real, ensure the danger was real. Julie didn't feel crazy, but was crazy something you could feel?

"You just seem a little, I don't know, tense or something. Everything okay?"

"Yeah, everything is great."

"You didn't have a fight with Sally, did you?"

"No, of course not. What's wrong with you? I'm fine."

"Okay, okay, sorry."

"You have to stop trying to read my moods all the time. I'm not a mental patient, at least not anymore, and you're not my doctor," Julie said.

"Sorry," Ryan apologized again. "You're absolutely right. I'm only trying to make sure you're okay."

"Well you have to stop. It's suffocating me."

"I know. I promise to be better."

"Can we go out for dinner? I don't want to cook."

"Feel like Italian?"

"You read my mind," Julie said.

The waitress placed a bowl of black tiger shrimp fettuccini in front of Julie, and the creamy dijon sauce wafted up from the plate. It smelled delicious. Ryan had ordered the seafood dish with the marinara sauce, as he always did. This was *their* restaurant, the place they had been coming to for years and a place they hadn't been back to since before Kayla was born. The woman who always seemed to serve them asked about the new baby. Julie was honest and told the woman Kayla had died in an accident. The exchange was awkward, and the woman said how sorry she was. Julie rubbed her shoulder and told her not to worry, they were going to try again. She turned and looked at Ryan. She hadn't seen him cry in a long time.

"Thanks for coming here with me," Julie said.

"It's nice to be back," said Ryan.

"After my visit with Sally I went on the net," Julie confessed.

"And?"

"And I looked up psychics and energy workers." Julie watched Ryan's face cloud over with scepticism and annoyance. Ryan was a dentist, his father had been an engineer, his mother a medical lab technician—his belief system revolved around science and logic. Julie could tell the mere mention of the word psychic had caused his rationality to flare up.

"Listen, I know what you're thinking, but hear me out first. What if the doctors are wrong? What if Dr. Pratt is wrong? What if these people in my dreams are real?"

Ryan rubbed his temples, his expression morphing from outright cynicism to hospital-faced concern. She was tempted again to tell him about Lindsay and Margo, but something held her back. It was the feeling that, if she told him, she would quickly wind up back in the hospital.

"I contacted a psychic trained as a Reiki master and—"

"Reiki master," interrupted Ryan. "I don't even know what the hell that is."

"She moves energy around and can heal you with her hands."

"Horseshit," said Ryan, tossing his fork down in frustration.

"Listen, I know this goes against pretty much everything you believe in, but I can't explain and can't get rid of these dreams. I can rationally say they are some sort of manifestation of my guilt about my brother and Kayla, but I'm still having the dreams. And what if these people are real and what if they're in danger and I'm the only one who can help them?"

Ryan sighed. "So, what, this psychic is going to help you find them so you can tell them, 'Excuse me, my psychic helped me track you down. If you're thinking of air travel in the near future, I might suggest the bus.'"

"No, she doesn't have to find them. I just want to go see her to see if maybe there's another explanation."

"Like what, dead people trying to contact you in your dreams?"

"Ryan, please, I don't know. I only want to see if she can help me get rid of them. Therapy hasn't worked, drugs haven't worked, not even time has slowed them down. It's been over four years now and the dreams are the most intense they've ever been. I want them to go away and maybe she can help me."

"What's this woman's name?"

"Zola," she said, prepared for the mockery Ryan was sure to unleash.

"Zola? She sounds like a gypsy fortune teller you'd find at the county fair. The great and mysterious Madame Zola. Come into my tent and allow me to gaze into my crystal ball and unlock the secrets of your future." Ryan placed his elbows on the table and held his head in his hands. He looked across the table at Julie. She didn't say anything.

"Fine," he said, leaning back. "You know what? I'm tired. Dead tired. I'm sure you must be too. And if you think Madame Zola can possibly help you out, then who am I to say differently? If you believe, well then maybe I should too."

5

It was a modest looking red brick bungalow. Each side of the walkway leading up to it was flanked with manicured shrubs, some of which had been covered with wooden slats for protection from the snow. The contemporary front door spoke of a recent renovation, and when Julie rang the doorbell it chimed with modern elegance. The door swung open and a woman who appeared to be in her mid-thirties answered the door in a simple white cotton dress and sandals. Her hair was thick and brown and hung loosely about her shoulders. Aside from the sandals, she didn't look anything like Julie had imagined. In fact, hers was closer to Ryan's stereotype—a scarf-sporting gypsy with hoop earrings and a wart on the end of her nose. Perhaps this was her daughter?

"You must be Julie," said the woman, smiling. "I'm Zola, please come in. Here, let me take your coat."

Julie looked about. The home was clean, sparse, with white walls and an open concept. Only a few pieces of art covered the walls, but they were striking, almost surreal photographs blown up to life size. One was of a man, in nothing but a pig mask, being pelted with raw eggs; the yolks, frozen in time and space, smeared across his mask and torso. It was a haunting and disturbing image and it greeted Julie in the main hallway.

Zola watched her stare at the painting. "Do you like it?"

"I would call it grotesquely beautiful," Julie said.

"You're different," Zola said, stepping around while continuing to observe her. It suddenly dawned on Julie, then, the purpose of the photograph. A distraction. Something to hold the client's attention while Zola gauged them, summed them up with whatever clairvoyant powers she might possess.

"How do you mean, different?" asked Julie, switching her gaze to her host.

"I mean very different. In fact I've never seen anything quite like it."

"What are you talking about?"

"Oh, I'm sorry, I don't mean to make you feel uncomfortable or nervous. I read people's energies. For me, these appear as colours around you. That's not exactly accurate, but it's the easiest way I can describe it. And you have the most wonderfully strange and intense colours I've ever seen."

"Is this good or bad?" Julie asked.

"I think it can be nothing but good. Energy is life and you're full of life. In fact you have enough for three lives."

Julie was stunned, but tried to keep her excitement in check. Could this woman, who was almost her age, really have extra sensory perception? But then again, maybe Julie did too. After all, that was why she was here.

"Why did you say three?" asked Julie. She watched as Zola continued to circle around her. Was she putting on some sort or act? In her email, Julie had deliberately left out any information about Lindsay or Margo and hadn't mentioned anything about her nightmares.

"That's how much energy I see, and it's almost as if there are three different people inside you. Actually, let me rephrase that. I see your energy and it's one colour, but then I see two other colours intertwined with yours. It's like you carry spirits with you," said Zola as she came to a stop in front of Julie. Normally Julie would be turned off by such odd behaviour, but today she wasn't. Instead she found herself excited by the prospect of finally having some sort of confirmation she wasn't insane after all, that Lindsay and Margo could really be the people from her dreams and that they might be in real danger.

"I must apologize again," said Zola. "This is not how I usually make an introduction. Even if I see something out of the ordinary, I usually keep it to myself. Please, come downstairs to my studio," she said, leading Julie to the stairs. Julie noted how quiet her footsteps were, almost as if she were floating across the hardwood floor. She followed Zola down the brightly lit staircase into a room lit by just a few candles. Along the far wall resided various religious artifacts highlighted by a large, colourful Aztec Sun Stone almost five feet in diameter flanked by numerous statues of the Buddha. Farther along were a collection of African masks, followed by a series of sceptres and sticks adorned with feathers and bound with leather straps. On the left was a collection of crosses of all sizes and denominations, some made of stone, and others of wood and metal. There were several stars of David, as well as a variety of voodoo dolls. This was what Julie had expected, but not in the manner in which Zola presented it. This was clinical, scientific, clean. It gave Julie the impression that this woman not only had a deep interest in the occult, the supernatural, and the afterlife, but a great reverence for the subject matter itself. This was no travelling circus act, no carnival show. This was the real deal.

"Please, have a seat," said Zola, guiding Julie to a small round table encircled by four straight-backed chairs. A massage table stood nearby.

"What's that for?"

"That's where I balance my client's energies," Zola said, and Julie nodded. She thought this sounded flaky, but then again Zola saw the energy fields of three people around her. Julie asked herself, Do I merely want to believe, or is this for real?

Zola took the chair opposite. She sat down slowly, with control, her back straight, her shoulders back. Zola had perfect posture. Her face was serene, conveying a sense of trust. Julie hadn't noticed it when she first came in, but now, seated here before Zola, it put her at ease and made her doubts all but vanish.

"Show me your hands please." Julie obliged, and held them out palms up before flipping them over so that Zola could see the backs too. "Rest them on the table palms up, please." Once again, Julie obeyed. Zola leaned forward. "May I touch you?" Julie nodded. Zola pressed her thumbs into the middle of Julie's palms and gripped her hands firmly. She closed her eyes. She remained like this, eyes closed, clutching Julie's hands for several minutes. Julie wondered what she could possibly be doing.

Without warning Zola stood up, causing her chair to fall over behind her. Then, her eyes firmly shut and her hands holding Julie's, she began to mumble softly.

"Sorry, what?" asked Julie, confused.

The mumbling grew louder. Zola was now speaking a language Julie didn't recognize. It sounded like gibberish.

"Please, you're scaring me," said Julie, trying to pull her hands away, but Zola's hands were clamped on tight. The garbled nonsense increased in volume and tempo, rising to the cusp of shouting. Julie wondered if this was really happening, or if perhaps she was dreaming. Was this an act? She didn't think so. The terror she felt was certainly real.

Zola stopped and opened her eyes. "They're going to die," she said calmly. Then she let go of Julie's hands, grabbed her head and screamed. Julie nearly toppled over in her chair. Not since her time in the hospital had she been so scared. She turned away, covering her ears with her hands. Finally the screaming came to an abrupt end and Zola collapsed to the floor. Julie rushed to her side.

"Zola, are you okay?" she asked. Zola's eyelids fluttered rapidly as she came to, disoriented. Julie helped her sit up.

"Are you okay?" Julie repeated.

"Yes, yes, I'm fine. Thank you," Zola said, lifting herself from the floor to sit unsteadily on one of the chairs. "I saw some things, horrible things. Julie, do you see them?"

"See who?"

"A young girl with blonde hair accompanied by a woman, maybe her mother?"

Julie nodded, overwhelmed with emotion.

"Julie, these two people are connected to you. You are their medium."

"What? What does that mean?"

Zola breathed heavily, speaking quickly. "You are connected. It's their energy I see around you."

Julie waited for more. "You said they were going to die," she said at length.

"Did I? I'm not sure. There was smoke and fire and screaming," said Zola, shaking her head.

"Can I save them?"

"I don't know," Zola said. "I just don't know."

6

When Ryan picked Julie up, she lied. He asked how it went, whether Zola had confirmed her dreams. Julie told him what he wanted to hear. She said Zola was a fruitcake, a side show of the bizarre, and she apologized for wasting his time and their money on something so silly. She knew if she told him the truth he wouldn't believe her and she didn't want to go back to the psychiatric ward. As much as she loved and trusted him, she needed to handle this on her own. It wasn't rational. Even she didn't fully accept it, so how could she expect Ryan to? Spiritually connected, that's what Zola called it. How could this happen? Why her? The questions raced through her brain all night, and when she finally fell asleep it was the usual nightmare followed by the jolting awake of Lindsay screaming, "Save her!"

Ryan kissed Julie on the cheek, thanked her for driving him to work again, and told her to have a great day. She smiled and waved. When he'd disappeared through the revolving doors she drove straight to the YMCA.

It was slightly after 9:00 when she arrived. She decided to wait in the lobby. It might be a waste of time, she thought, but sitting in the South Keys parking lot had paid off so maybe this would too. The game began again, writing down descriptions of people pushing through the turnstile and noting the time. This was much easier, with fewer people, and she could see everyone going in and out. Now to sit and wait.

By three that afternoon Julie was exhausted and wanted to go home, but she remained focused and determined. She thought about what she was going to say. She imagined several different dialogues, from the weather to her daughter. In some conversations she described what happened to Kayla and pictured Lindsay's horrified and sympathetic reaction. Julie decided if she did get a chance to speak to Lindsay she wouldn't bring up her daughter or her brother. The most complicated part would be trying to explain to a complete stranger that Julie had been dreaming about her for years and that she might die in a plane crash. Every time she thought about initiating the conversation, it never sounded right in her head. It was like trying to sell someone on the existence of unicorns or extraterrestrials. Ridiculous. She would have to rely on her own sincerity to get the message home. If she was earnest enough, wouldn't Lindsay have to believe her? But Julie knew Sally and Ryan were right. She knew she couldn't just come out and say, "Hey, I've been dreaming about you for years and, by the way, you are going to die." It sounded completely mad. She would have to befriend her first, gain her trust before she said anything. She would have to wait and try again tomorrow; it was time to pick Ryan up from work.

"What's up, you seem off?" Julie took a bite of her Harvey's cheeseburger. Ryan looked up from stirring a French fry in a puddle of ketchup. He popped it into his mouth.

"It's nothing," he said, chewing.

"Obviously something's wrong. You've been acting weird since I picked you up. What's up?"

He looked her in the eye. "Sally called me at work."

"Jesus Christ, I told her not to. What did she say?"

"All she said was that she's really worried about you. Quite frankly, so am I."

"I'm fine. What else did she say?"

"That's all she said."

"Ryan, what else did she tell you?" Julie demanded. He sighed and remained silent.

"Did she tell you about the woman and the girl?"

"Yes," said Ryan.

"It's them, Ryan. I didn't tell you because I didn't think you'd believe me, but it's them. I saw them."

"You also saw them on the canal, remember?"

"No. That was a mistake. This is really them. And Zola, I lied about that too because again I didn't think you'd believe me, but she saw them too. The little girl and her mom are real, Ryan. Real," she said, grabbing his hand.

"I don't understand why you lied to me."

"I just told you—I didn't think you'd believe me."

"Listen, Julie, I think you're really sick and need to go to the hospital."

"Fuck! See?" said Julie. "I told Sally. Ryan, I swear on my life, these two are the ones from my dreams."

"Please, Julie," whispered Ryan, leaning in closer. "Do you know how crazy that sounds?"

"Yes I fucking know! That's exactly why I didn't tell you, because I knew if I did you'd have this reaction."

"Please, just let me take you to the hospital."

"I'm not going to any fucking hospital," Julie spat. A few heads turned and glanced over.

"I'm not going to the hospital," repeated Julie, lowering her voice to a whisper. "There's nothing wrong with me. I need you to believe me."

"Okay, but you need to go back on your medication. You can't drink. This is what happened the last time."

"I'm not drinking for Christ's sake."

"That's not what Sally told me."

Julie remembered the pub and shook her head defeatedly.

"Julie, please," continued Ryan. "At least make an appointment with Dr. Pratt."

"Fine, if it will make you happy, I will," she said, hoping this would be enough to placate him until she could find Lindsay. She didn't know if she had enough time. Something—maybe fate, or a divine force—had brought them together, and she needed to find her. "I need to save them," she said.

"You're the one who needs saving," said Ryan, "and I'm doing my best to do that. You're not making it easy."

Julie sensed an opportunity to shut the conversation down. All she needed was to convince him of her desire to get help, even though she hadn't the slightest intention of doing so.

"I promise to take my meds and I promise I'll make an appointment with Dr. Pratt tomorrow," she said flatly.

Ryan nodded. "Okay," he said, "I just want you to be okay."

The rest of the evening felt awkward as they both tiptoed around the subject of Julie's nightmares. Before bed she made sure Ryan heard her opening pill bottles and tapping out pills. She drank water out of the tap and tossed the pills into the toilet.

They kissed goodnight when she got into bed, and Ryan turned out the light. Julie listened to his rhythmic breathing while he slept. She thought about what she needed to do until she finally drifted off. She woke at 6:00AM screaming, the smell of burning jet fuel filling her nose.

7

There was a different homeless person standing near the entrance of the YMCA, a woman rocking side to side smoking a cigarette. Julie didn't make eye contact as she pushed through the doors into the warmth of the lobby. She plunked herself down with her gym bag, pulled out her notebook and began her journaling. And at that exact moment Lindsay walked in. Julie's heart began to race and her palms grew wet with perspiration. Everything she'd planned to do, every conversation starter she'd rehearsed, was immediately forgotten. She said nothing as Lindsay walked past, and Lindsay didn't notice her. She got up and followed her through the turnstile and into the locker room. She chose a locker a few feet down and began to change into her running clothes. She kept glancing over at Lindsay, trying not to be caught staring. Here she was again, in the flesh, confirming everything. Julie started when Lindsay caught her staring.

"Hey, it's you again," said Julie, smiling. Lindsay tilted her head in puzzlement. "I bumped into you a few days ago in the parking lot at South Keys. Literally bumped into you. You and your daughter."

"Oh, right," said Lindsay, smiling.

"I knew I recognized you from somewhere."

"Funny, I'm usually good at remembering faces, and I just don't recall seeing you here."

Julie shrugged. "I've only been a member a short time and I'm pretty forgettable."

This made Lindsay laugh as she swung her locker door closed. They sat there and tied their running shoes.

"Hey, is that an Ironman tattoo on your ankle?" asked Lindsay. She said it with a friendly curiosity Julie relished because she thought it might provide a way to continue the conversation.

"Good eye," said Julie, smiling. "I got it right after I finished. I think getting the tattoo hurt more than the race. I've only done one, so far."

"That's so cool. I'm hoping to qualify this spring for Boston."

"Really? That's great! I did Boston six years ago."

"Wow, you're my hero. Sorry, I think you told me your name but I forgot," said Lindsay.

"Julie," said Julie, extending her hand.

"Lindsay. Nice to run into you again."

"Let's go run," said Julie.

"Let's."

They talked all aspects of marathon running, from shoes to diet to training. Julie spewed her years of experience and Lindsay listened attentively. After forty minutes on the treadmill, they completed a double tour of the weight machines, their conversation continuing to flow naturally. Julie abandoned the notion of trying to warn Lindsay or mentioning anything about her dreams. It would come across as insane, and any chance to save her and her daughter would evaporate. No, she would wait, and only when she felt the time was right, only then would she even consider bringing it up.

"I see you wear a wedding ring," said Julie as they headed back downstairs to the change room.

"Oh that's Dan. I miss my Dan," said Lindsay, clutching her ring to her chest.

"Oh, I'm sorry," said Julie. "I didn't know. I shouldn't have pried."

Lindsay laughed. "Dan's not dead. He's in San Francisco. And don't be silly, you're not prying."

"Thank goodness," said Julie. "What's he doing there?"

"Helping set up the company that recently acquired his. He's been down there a month."

"Wow, that's cool. When does he get back?"

"Not for a while yet. But my daughter Margo and I are going to fly down Christmas morning."

Julie suddenly felt dizzy. Her knees began to buckle. "I need to sit down," she said, leaning against a locker.

"Here," Lindsay said, guiding her to a bench. "Are you okay?"

"I'm fine. I didn't eat anything this morning and I'm suddenly feeling lightheaded is all. I'll be okay in a minute."

"Let me get you some juice."

"No, no. I'm fine, really. Maybe it's because you said fly," said Julie, offering the most playful smile she could muster. "I hate flying. Terrified of it. Never recommend it, flying."

"Are you sure? I think you should have some juice."

"I'm okay, but you're right, I should really eat something. Would you care to join me for lunch?"

"I think I'd better," Lindsay said.

After showering, Lindsay asked Julie if she'd mind watching her things while she went to the bathroom. Julie took the opportunity to root through Lindsay's purse and find her wallet. After memorizing Lindsay's address, she slipped the wallet back in, took out her cellphone, and emailed it to herself.

"Ready to go?" Lindsay asked.

"Ready," Julie replied, hitting SEND.

Grounded Kitchen was crowded with the usual business bravado, but they still managed a table by the window. Giant portraits of John Lennon and Ray Charles gazed affectionately from the walls.

"It's like fate brought us together," said Lindsay later as she bit into her chicken and eggplant panini. She cooed with delight.

"Good eh?"

"So good. Thanks for bringing me. This place is pretty cool."

"Do you believe in that sort of thing? Fate?" Julie asked.

"Um, I'm not really sure. I believe in luck. Sometimes you get lucky—like meeting you. I think meeting you was luck more than fate. I don't know, maybe they're the same thing? I'm not sure what the difference is actually. Sorry. Rambling. I talk and think out loud. It drives Dan nuts."

"No, that's great," said Julie. "I think fate is what happens, and luck is what we attribute it to. But I think whatever's going to happen is going to happen, regardless."

"I think I follow what you're saying, but I also believe you make your own luck, your own fate. For example, if you work hard while training, eat the right food and stick to your race plan, then you get your qualifying time for Boston. In that case it's fate that you qualified, but it's a fate you have some control over, right?"

"Right," agreed Julie.

"But running into you, that's luck. Good luck."

"Right," said Julie again. "Good luck." She wanted to tell Lindsay everything—the dreams, Kayla, her brother, everything. She wanted to spill it all, but instead she picked up her fork, calmly took a bite of her salad, and smiled.

8

Their conversation was warm and growing more personal when Julie asked about Margo. Lindsay relayed funny stories about her daughter and confided that she went through fertility treatments to get pregnant; explained how lucky she felt to have her. When Lindsay asked Julie if she had any kids, Julie answered, "No. I mean we did have one, but she died in an accident."

"I'm so sorry," Lindsay said.

"Thanks. We're working on having another one." Julie didn't explain how Kayla had died and Lindsay didn't ask. It was always awkward, but this time it felt less so. With the disclosure of such personal and intimate subject matter, Julie suddenly felt very close to Lindsay.

They exchanged numbers after lunch as they walked back to their cars. Lindsay said she'd call when she got back from San Francisco so they could meet up and train together again. They hugged. For Julie, it was like hugging a sister she never had. She couldn't be sure, but she got the impression Lindsay felt the same way. She wondered if she could really trust her own emotions. She'd been living with this woman on an exploding aircraft for years. There was some sort of genuine connection between them, something almost tangible. Julie was feeling the pull and it was unbelievably strong, and in three days her new friend was going to board a plane with her daughter and probably die. Julie knew in her heart and soul this was true. She only had three days to figure out how to stop them from flying. Should she tell Lindsay about her dreams? Maybe she could get her husband to fly up here instead? But how would she ever be able to pull that off? Impossible. No, stopping them from getting on the plane in the first place seemed to be the only option. But how?

Three days. The risk of telling Lindsay about her dreams was too much. If it backfired, if she came off sounding crazy—and how could she not—it would only put distance between them. But was there any other option? If Lindsay thought she was crazy, she would get on the plane. If Julie told her, Lindsay would think she was crazy. If Julie didn't tell her, Lindsay would get on the plane. Either way, she'd get on the plane, and die.

Julie was thinking about different scenarios when she pulled up in front of her house to find a police car parked in the driveway. That's odd, she thought, walking up the steps, kicking at the snow on the edges as she went. When she walked through the door, she stomped her feet on the mat and looked up to find Ryan, Sally, her husband Rich and his brother, the police officer, standing in the living room waiting for her.

"Hi honey," said Ryan. He was supposed to be at work for the next three hours. Julie knew from his tone, knew from the people standing before her, that this was some sort of intervention. Sally had turned her in, ever the dutiful friend. Julie should have seen this coming. If she thought a friend was crazy, wouldn't she turn her in to get the help she needed? Of course she would. She wasn't crazy and nobody except Zola and Lil believed her. With so much on the line and so little time left, how could she talk her way out of this?

"What are you doing here?" Julie asked.

Sally cupped her chin and mouth as she had in the pub, deeply saddened about what was happing to her friend.

"We've been talking about you and we think it might be best if you went back to the hospital for a while," Ryan said. His voice trembled when he spoke, amplifying the tension in the room.

"Ryan, they're real and I have to save them. They're getting on a plane in three days and we have to stop them. It fact, we should stop the plane. Everyone on that plane is going to die and we have to prevent it. Maybe we can call the airline or something? I don't know what to do, but they can't get on that plane. You guys can help me, right? It's Peter, right?" Julie asked the officer.

Peter nodded.

"Okay, Peter here can call the airline and tell them not to take off because of some sort of terror threat, right?"

"Sweetie, you need to go back to the hospital because you're sick and you need to get help," Ryan said. Sally nodded as Rich and Peter looked on with sympathetic expressions. Julie stepped into the room without taking off her boots.

"Please, don't do this. I'm begging you. You're going to kill everyone on that plane if you don't help me stop it. Please, I'm not crazy. It sounds crazy, but it's real. Please, help me."

"You can come with me voluntarily," said Peter, "or we can go the other way. Regardless, you have to come with me, because I have a court order to bring you in for a psychiatric assessment. Do you understand?"

"Court order? How?"

"I got it," said Ryan meekly.

"Why would you do that? How could you not believe me?"

"Because it's all in your head," Sally interjected.

"Do you want to grab a toothbrush and some pyjamas before we go?" Peter asked.

"I thought it was just an assessment? What makes you think I'm going to stay?" Julie asked, her voice rising, almost shouting. The radio on Peter's belt crackled with the garbled voice of another officer. He pinched the small microphone on his left shoulder and spoke into it. "10-19 with EMH, caution echo, request additional officer. See if Judy is around."

"10-4," chirped a voice.

"So, Ryan, why don't you get her a few things she needs and meet us there," Peter said.

"Okay," said Ryan, not moving.

"I'm not going anywhere," Julie yelled. "You got that? People are going to die and we need to help them. Now just stop this right now!"

Nobody moved. Instead they just stood and stared at Julie until she felt hot and dizzy. Jesus Christ, could this really be happening? Not now, not when she was so close to saving them.

"It's for your own good," squeaked Sally eventually.

"My own good? My own fucking good? Jesus Christ, Sally, you promised me, and now look at this. If these people die, you, and you, and you, and you," Julie said, thrusting her finger at each of them, "will be responsible for their deaths. Do you understand what I'm saying? I'm not fooling around here. This is truly a matter of life and death."

They all remained silent.

"I'm afraid it's time to go," said Peter at length.

"Well I'm not going," said Julie, defiantly crossing her arms. She looked at Ryan for support but he looked down at the floor. Julie heard a car pull up outside. She turned and looked out the window to see a second police cruiser. A female officer was getting out. This must be Judy, Julie thought. A knock on the door and Peter told her to come in.

"We're on our way out—right, Julie?" Peter said, walking toward her and the door.

"Okay, fine, let's go," she said, putting her hands up. "Do you mind if I get my toothbrush and stuff?"

"Go ahead," said Peter. "We'll wait right here."

Julie ascended the stairs, made her way down the hall to the bedroom, and quietly shut the door. As she cranked open the window the cold air blew a fine spray of snow into her face. After popping out the screen, she looked down at the slanted, snow-covered roof of the addition. Only six feet, but she needed to be quiet. And fast. She tore off the bedsheets, and tied one around the bedpost. With her feet resting on the foot of the bed, she leaned back holding the sheet, testing the sheet's strength. It held, and so she tied the other sheet to the first and pulled hard. "Here we go," she whispered to herself. Out the window she climbed feet first, clutching the sheet. Her legs slipped down the side of the cold brick until the bottom of her ribcage rested on the window sill. Suddenly she felt the bed slide. It made a horrible screeching sound, and she quickly slid to the end of the sheet and let go. When she landed on the addition, she bent her knees and compressed down into a ball as softly as she could, making the least amount of noise possible. She looked down and jumped into the snow of the backyard. She landed awkwardly and twisted her ankle. As she stood, she saw Peter appear at her bedroom window. She turned and ran, ignoring the pain in her ankle.

Scrambling over the fence, she limped down the alleyway between the houses towards her neighbour's backyard. When she came out onto the adjoining street, the second cruiser was rounding the corner. Julie bolted across the road and ran between the next set of houses. A dog barked on the other side of a fence, running alongside her until she emerged on the next street and ran towards Bank Street in hope of losing them in a Christmas crowd of shoppers. She only made it half a block before Peter's cruiser rounded the corner and blocked the road. Julie turned to find the second cruiser doing the same thing at the other end of the block. There was nowhere to go. She knew it was over. She limped to Peter's car. Nothing was said as he opened the door and guided her in, lightly touching the top of her head.

9

There was an awkward silence in the waiting room as Julie, Ryan, Sally, Rich, and Peter waited for her to be seen by the resident. When she came in, Peter talked to the doctor first. Julie assumed he was explaining how insane she was and why they needed to keep her here indefinitely. Ryan got up and joined them. How could he not have her back when she needed him most? Julie watched as the doctor, who looked to be in her mid-twenties, disappeared into a room with the two men and shut the door behind them. A few minutes later Peter reappeared. He told Rich and Sally he was going to go. "Good luck," he said to Julie.

"Thanks for all your hard work, Peter," she said.

"We're only trying to help," said Sally.

"I'm not the one who needs help," snapped Julie. The door to the room opened again and Ryan and the doctor stepped back into the waiting room.

"Okay, Julie, would you care to join me?" asked the doctor.

Not really, thought Julie as she entered the small room and took a seat on the chair next to the examination table. The doctor sat across from her.

"I'm Doctor Rangan," she said, holding steady eye contact. "And you're Julie Cooper, correct?"

"How old are you?"

"I turned thirty yesterday," said Dr. Rangan. Her voice was calm, and the question didn't seem to faze her.

"Happy birthday," said Julie.

"Thank you. I've looked over your file here. You've been under the care of Dr. Pratt, correct?"

Julie nodded.

"And you were discharged two weeks ago?"

"Yes."

The doctor looked up from her file and resumed eye contact. Julie wondered if this was part of her training, or whether she was just naturally good with people.

"So tell me, why are you here today?"

"I'm here today because the people out there in the waiting room think I'm crazy and should be locked up in this psychiatric facility."

"And you don't think you should be?"

"No, of course not."

"Can you tell me a little about what's been happening since you left the hospital?"

"Not much. Doing a little Christmas shopping."

"That's nice. Anything else? Would you care to explain to me why your husband and your friend have brought you in here? They seem to be quite concerned about you."

"What did they tell you?"

"They're concerned you might try to hurt yourself again."

Julie laughed and slapped her knee. Dr. Rangan didn't react, merely maintained eye contact.

"Ridiculous!" spat Julie. "Simply ridiculous. Listen, doctor, there was never really a suicide attempt, or whatever it says in my file there, it was an accidental overdose. I mixed some pills with some alcohol and passed out in a car. I mean, it sounds bad, right? I admit I wasn't thinking clearly, but killing myself was never on the agenda. Never. And if you ask me if I'm suicidal now, the answer is absolutely not. I feel great. Never better."

"Your husband told me you haven't been taking your medication and you've been drinking again. Is that true?"

"I had some wine with dinner."

"If I ordered a blood test for you right now, would I see the correct levels of medication?"

"Absolutely," Julie lied. She thought the doctor was bluffing. She'd never order a blood test.

"Can you tell me about these dream people you've been seeing?"

Julie sighed, rubbed her face with her hands and then rubbed her palms together like she was trying to keep warm.

"Okay," she said, "here we go." She explained everything quickly and earnestly; how four years of dreaming had led to this.

"So you see," she concluded, "I have to save them. I have to figure out how to prevent them from getting on that plane."

"Here is the thing, Julie. You seem pretty sane to me. Would you consider staying with us on a voluntary basis over the holidays?" asked Dr. Rangan.

"Didn't you hear what I said? Why would you want me to stay here after I told you all that?"

"Julie, do you think it's possible that Lindsay and her daughter Margo will get on that plane on Christmas morning and be perfectly fine?"

"No, they're going to die. Everyone on that plane is going to die."

"Are you going to be on that plane?"

"No, of course not."

"And yet in your dream you're on the plane."

"So?"

"So, what I'm getting at is not everything in your dream is true, correct?"

"Well I have to be there to have a vision, don't I?"

"But you won't be on the plane?"

"No."

"Then maybe it's possible it won't blow up? How do you know it's this flight and not the return flight from San Francisco, or even some other flight?"

"I don't know."

"Then it's possible, just possible, that the plane might not blow up, correct?"

"Maybe, but do I want to take that chance?"

"Will you consider staying with us on a voluntary basis?"

"No," said Julie firmly.

"Okay, well I'm afraid you're going to have to stay with us whether you want to or not."

"I'm not staying," said Julie, standing up. The doctor was saying something but Julie didn't hear—she was focused on the door. She was angry. The sound of her heartbeat throbbed in her ears. Ryan, Sally and Rich turned their heads and watched her make for the exit. Julie heard Ryan ask where she was going. She ignored him and continued to walk down the hall toward the sliding doors of the exit when she heard over PA system, "Code Grey. All available orderlies to emergency. Code Grey." She heard the sounds of running behind her. Two orderlies appeared around a corner before her.

"Easy now," one of them said, motioning for her to stop. Glancing over her shoulder, she saw two more running down the hallway toward her. She bolted at them, diving between the larger man's legs. To her surprise, she managed to slide right through, her momentum carrying her well past where she sprang to her feet and continued running. It was happening so fast, yet time seemed to slow for her. She could hear her own breathing as she pumped her legs toward the exit doors. Suddenly a man appeared in front of her, and they collided. They both fell to the floor. Julie managed to gather her legs under her and was almost up again when she felt a hand grab her coat. Another hand grabbed her wrist. She was forced back to the floor. "Get the fuck off of me!" she screamed.

"Take it easy," said the orderly holding her. Julie fought with everything she had. "Don't do that," he said as she tried to bite him.

"We got a rabid one here," said another. "We need a shot ASAP." Julie spit at him just as Dr. Rangan appeared, needle in hand.

"Hold her as still as possible," she ordered.

"Don't do this, you'll kill them! Don't you understand? I have to save them. They will die if you do this!" Julie pleaded as out of the corner of her eye she saw Ryan. He looked horrified.

"Please, Ryan, don't let them do this. You're going to kill them. I need to save her!"

She felt the prick of the needle, and a few seconds later her muscles went limp and her vision blurred.

"Wait a minute," she slurred as they placed her in a wheelchair and rolled her away.

10

The smell of bleach and the trickling sound of water being wrung out in a mop bucket; the wet smacking sound of the ropey tassels hitting the floor. Somebody was cleaning. She opened her eyes slowly. She was in a bed in a windowless room in the hospital. This was the most secure ward. No glass to break, nothing to cut yourself with, nothing to jump out of. Here you were safe from yourself, at least as safe as they could make it, but people got creative when they were serious about leaving. During her previous stay on the other floor, she heard about a woman who'd used a bed sheet, tied one end to the doorknob and threw the other end over the door—she managed to hang herself with less than half an inch between her toes and the ground. Julie had no such plans. Her first thoughts were of escape, but her head was in a fog. How long had she been here? How long had she been out? She sat up slowly and swung her feet to the floor. The room spun with her, almost like she was drunk, minus the nausea. Her mind was slow and her mouth was dry cotton. The meds they dosed her with were strong, much stronger than anything she'd had before. She noticed she was wearing her blue pajamas. Ryan must have brought them. She stood up and held onto the wall for support. "Wow," she muttered, surprised by her wonky physical and mental state. "Son of a bitch," she slurred and drooled. She watched her spittle hang off her lip; got lost staring at the shiny gooey tendril. It eventually broke off and landed on her bare foot. "Huh, look at that. I'm drooling," she mumbled. She shook her head trying to clear the murkiness, but it only made her dizzy. Lurching toward the door, using the wall for support, she was determined to get out. She expected the door to be locked, but the knob turned freely in her hand and swung open when pushed. In the hallway a man was mopping the floor. He glanced at her briefly and then went back to his job, whistling gleefully.

Her feet felt cold on the floor, but the chill provided a welcome sobering effect to her groggy state of mind. She wandered to the nurses' station next to the elevator where a nurse she didn't recognize was typing. Julie stood and stared at her. She didn't pay any attention to Julie. After a minute or so the nurse stopped typing and looked up at Julie. "Yes, how can I help you?"

"I need to make a phone call."

"No calls after 8:00 I'm afraid."

"What time is it?"

"Almost 2:00AM. Nice to see you up. You've been down for some time."

"How long?"

"Pretty long."

"What day is it?"

"Well, since it's now 2:00 in the morning, it's technically Christmas Eve."

"They leave tomorrow and I'm locked up in here."

"Who's that?"

"Santa and his flying reindeer," Julie deadpanned. The nurse didn't react. "When can I make a phone call?" Julie asked.

"8:00AM."

"Thank you," said Julie. She wandered over to the water fountain and drank her fill, even though she wasn't all that thirsty and the water tasted metallic. She returned to her room and lay down on the floor. Looking up at the ceiling, she thought about what she needed to do. First, though, she managed an awkward sit up. Then she did another. And another. After twenty, her pace picked up. After a hundred, she flipped over and did a hundred pushups. Sweat formed along her forearms, breasts, and face. She got up, went down the hall to the bathroom, and took a piss. On the way back she stooped and drank heavily once again from the fountain. Whatever medication they had her on, she was determined to burn it out of her system. Callisthenics followed by yoga were next on the agenda. And plenty of water. She needed to flush the system clean.

At 7:59AM she was standing at the nursing desk. It was shift change and she knew the nurse coming on.

"Good Morning, Claire," she said, smiling. "Welcome to work."

"Good lord, Julie, what are you doing back here? Why are you on this floor?"

"Apparently I've got a screw loose," answered Julie. It made Claire laugh.

"I'm sorry to hear that," said Claire, continuing to chuckle.

"Listen, I need to make a phone call," said Julie, doing her best to sound cheerful.

"Sure, you look really sweaty. You okay?" Claire asked, passing Julie the phone.

"I feel much better than when I woke up."

The night nurse put on her coat to leave. "Ready to go Jill?" Claire asked.

"Ready," Jill replied. Julie watched Claire push a button under the counter, summoning the elevator.

"Merry Christmas, Jill. Have a good holiday if I don't see you," said Claire.

"You too," said Jill as the elevator door opened and she stepped inside.

Julie flipped open the phone, but couldn't remember the number. Shit. She'd just had it in her head.

"I need to use the phone," said a man, appearing at her side. He had scraggly grey hair with a matching beard and he stunk of cigarettes. "Please, I need to use the phone. I need to call the FBI."

"No, Carl, you can't have the phone. Remember? No phone for two weeks," said Claire.

"Please," Carl persisted. "I really need to call the FBI and the CIA. Please."

"Carl, leave Julie alone to make her call please."

Eventually Carl wandered off, and Julie completed her call. Then she returned to her room and shut the door. Now she would just have to wait.

11

The elevator doors opened and out stepped a girl in black army boots sprouting ripped fishnets that crawled up her legs only to disappear under a tight black miniskirt. The black hoodie she wore was lightly dusted with snow and a strip of green hair stuck out like an overgrowing vine. She pulled back the hood and shook her head as a wet dog would.

"It's fucking cold outside," she said.

"Lil, what are you doing here?" asked Claire.

"Came to see my imprisoned friend."

"Hey!" Julie shouted from down the hallway. "I'm so happy you could make it."

Claire watched as Lil and Julie embraced.

"Let's stroll," Julie said.

"Let's," said Lil. The two wandered down the hallway to Julie's room. Once inside, both women began to disrobe.

"Think this is going to work?" Lil asked.

"It's the only shot I've got, so it's got to," said Julie. "Did Zola bring you?"

"Waiting for you downstairs."

After the women had swapped clothes, Julie asked, "So how do I look?"

"Hot," said Lil. "Now let's do your makeup and nails." Lil pulled a bottle of black nail polish and a black lipstick from her bra and went to work on Julie. Twenty minutes later Lil stood back and proudly declared her a masterpiece. Julie looked at herself in the dark reflection of Lil's mobile phone.

"I look like a member of The Cure."

Lil frowned. "What's The Cure?"

"Never mind. Pass me your boots."

"You're funny," said Lil, removing her boots.

"Fuck, these are tight."

"Quit complaining. Okay, pull the hoodie over your head."

"Well," asked Julie, pulling the hood down as far as she could, "am I believable?"

"You look great. You look like me," said Lil, smiling.

"Okay, here goes nothing." Julie stepped toward the door.

"Wait."

"What?"

"Why are you leaving so soon?"

Julie thought about it for a second. "Because I forgot your Christmas gift in the car?"

"Nicely played. Good luck."

"Thanks for doing this, Lil."

"I'm only doing it because I believe you. Besides, I can always plead insanity. Go save some lives."

Julie winked, opened the door and headed down the hallway toward the elevator where Claire sat busily at her computer. Carl and another patient came lurching down the hall toward her. Fuck, she thought, and kept her head down. When she arrived at the elevator, she mumbled at Claire, "Buzz me down? Forgot Julie's Christmas gift."

"You sound like you're catching a cold. You should wear something warmer," Claire said, reaching under the counter to summon the elevator.

"Excuse me," said Carl, coming up to Julie. "Do you have a phone? I need to call the FBI."

"No," she growled. "Get away from me."

"Carl, leave Lil alone please," ordered Claire.

"It's not Lil. You said her name was Julie," Carl mumbled just as the elevator doors opened and Julie stepped in and hit the button for the ground floor. Her heart thumped in her chest. The elevator wasn't moving.

"That's Julie," said Carl, pointing into the elevator.

Why isn't this fucking thing closing, Julie thought as she hit the close button repeatedly. Just as the doors began to shut, Carl's sidekick stuck his arm in, and the doors clunked to a stop and slid back to their open position again.

"Excuse me, Bobby, you need to let the elevator go, okay?" said Claire. Julie couldn't see Claire, but suspected she was going to emerge from behind the desk. Sure enough she heard the rolling of the chair, and Julie looked down at the uncomfortable boots she was wearing and held her breath. Shit, come on, she thought, and hit the close button again. Claire appeared just as the doors began to close again, and once more the man named Bobby blocked them. He stared at Julie as though she were possessed by a demon.

"Why does Julie get to leave?" asked Carl. Claire glanced into the elevator.

"That's Lil," she said. "Now please, move along."

The doors began to close and this time Bobby left them alone. Julie watched his face disappear behind the door, and when the elevator finally began to descend she exhaled. In the lobby she didn't make eye contact with anyone; she simply marched to the exit, stepped outside into lightly falling snow, and found Zola waiting in her car in the spot they had agreed upon.

"You look lovely," said Zola.

"You're hilarious. Thanks for doing this."

"Where are we going?"

"My house in the Glebe," said Julie. "I need to get some stuff, like a change of clothes. Can I borrow your phone?"

"My purse in the backseat."

Julie found it, and on the third ring a voiced answered, "Hello."

"Hi, Lindsay. It's me, Julie."

"Oh hi. I didn't think I'd hear from you until after I was back."

"Sorry, I don't mean to bother you. Are you in the middle of something?"

"No, nothing. I mean, just packing for tomorrow, but it's fine. I'm happy you called. I really enjoyed our lunch the other day."

"Well, I was wondering if I could come by quickly and drop off a small gift for Margo?"

"For sure. Come anytime, we're just hanging out."

"Great. I'll swing by this afternoon then."

12

Julie scrunched down in the seat as they rolled down her block. "Is the car in the driveway?"

"No, and the lights are off in the house. Looks like he isn't home."

"He might have gone to work or he might be on his way to see me at the hospital. I'll be quick," said Julie, sitting up. "Honk twice if he shows."

Julie noticed what appeared to be fairly fresh boot prints in the snow on the stairs. They were leading away from the house, and they matched the timeline of the tire tracks in the driveway. If Ryan had left only a short time ago, he probably went to the hospital. It wouldn't be long before they discovered her deception. She had to be quick. Under the planter on the porch she found the spare key, and in she went. The warmth and smell of home wafted about her as she stepped into the front hall. The WELCOME HOME banner still hung in the window next to the Christmas tree. A fresh wave of doubt washed over her. What if she was wrong? What if they were destined to die and there was nothing she could do to stop it? But Lil was sitting in the hospital and Zola was waiting in the car outside, on Christmas Eve. It must mean something. With this in mind, Julie bolted up the stairs. In her bedroom she undressed and hid Lil's clothes under the bed. She threw on a red dress and black tights and pulled her hair into a ponytail. In the bathroom she reached behind the toilet and found the bottle of sleeping medication she'd hidden. Then she grabbed the Gravol from the medicine cabinet.

She stepped back into the bedroom and saw it hanging there above the bed—the Ojibwe dream-catcher Ryan had given her over three years before. Perfect, she thought, and went to the hall closet to find a gift bag and red tissue. She wrapped the dream-catcher neatly in the tissue and placed it in the bag. Downstairs she found her purse. She tossed in her medication and grabbed a bottle of wine from the rack in the kitchen.

She put on an old coat, one she had meant to donate but hadn't yet. Her good one was at the hospital along with her boots. Shit. She couldn't wear Lil's combat boots again. Julie rooted through the hall closet until she found her purple rain boots with white polka dots. "You'll have to do," she said, slipping them on. She was about to head back out the door when she remembered the package of hot chocolate she had sitting in the spice cabinet, part of a gift basket she'd won at work. Perfect, she thought as she tossed it into the bag.

Outside, the snow had stopped. As she came down her walkway she heard Zola start up the car.

Zola sat in the car once again as Julie disappeared through the revolving doors. In the lobby a security guard sat at his desk reading a newspaper. He didn't look up as Julie crossed his path and made her way to the elevator. She hopped in and hit 5.

The silver plate on the door read DR. RYAN CHARLAND AND DR. MATT KERBY. Above it a note was taped, stating that the office was closed for the holidays. Julie found the key on her chain and popped it into the lock. The alarm sounded its warning. She stepped inside and punched the code into the pad.

She moved across the waiting room and through the little door to the receptionist's desk. The key for the medicine cabinet was in the top drawer. She pulled on the handle but it refused to budge. She yanked on the handle again, this time harder, shaking it. "Jesus Christ," she said. She went down the hall to the back room where she knew Ryan kept a small tool kit. She grabbed the hammer and returned to the desk, stabbed its claw into the top of the drawer and pulled. The metal bent slightly, but the drawer remained in place. Julie grabbed a stapler off the desk and stuck it behind the hammer's head for leverage. Then she tried again, managing to slowly separate the drawer from the desk. Finally she ripped it open with both hands.

Armed with the keys, she opened the medicine cabinet. "Diazepam Tablets," she said, reading the label. She shook the bottle gleefully, then popped the top and spilled some pills onto the counter. Grabbing some scissors, she cut off all five fingers of a rubber glove found in a box mounted on the wall. In each rubber digit she deposited various combinations of Diazepam, Gravol, and sleeping pills. Holding the end of a finger shut to keep the contents from flying out, Julie carefully hammered the pills until they were powder. She repeated this for the other four fingers, and tied the opened ends with elastics. She put the three strong doses in her right pocket and the two weak ones in her left.

On the way out she reset the alarm. Down in the lobby the security guard was still reading his paper; he barely gave her a glance as she hurried past. Outside, Zola sat waiting in the car.

"Get what you needed?"

Julie nodded.

"Radio says we might be in for a big snowstorm. Forty to sixty centimeters," Zola said.

"When?"

"Tomorrow night."

"They're scheduled to fly tomorrow morning."

"Things get delayed all the time. Maybe this is what happens?"

"I've never dreamt about snow."

"What season is it in your dream?"

"I don't know, I've never thought about it before. Funny, I always thought it was summer," Julie said, pinching her lower lip.

"Are you sure you want to do this?" Zola asked.

Julie nodded, and they drove in silence all the way to Pleasant Park Road.

"Want me to wait?" Zola asked.

"No, go enjoy your family. It's Christmas Eve," Julie said.

Julie reached for the door handle and Zola grabbed her arm. "Wait. Maybe we should go to the police."

"Not to state the obvious, but a psychic and an escaped mental patient walk into the police station . . . I mean, it even sounds like a joke."

"But what are you going to do?"

"Stop them from getting on the plane tomorrow."

"But how?"

Julie shrugged. "Any way I can, I suppose."

13

Even though the walkway leading up to the door had recently been cleared of snow, a thin hardened layer of white ice remained. Salt crystals and sand coated the surface, and Julie's boots crunched as she walked up the path. Through the window she saw a Christmas tree decorated with white lights and ornaments. Frank Sinatra could be heard offering holiday cheer. She rang the bell and seconds later the door flung open, revealing Margo.

"Enter our castle," the little girl exclaimed as Lindsay came scooting down the hall in an apron.

"Come in, come in," she said, waving Julie in.

"Are you my mom's new friend?" Margo asked.

"Margo, don't be rude."

"How is that rude?" Margo frowned.

"Well, I suppose I am," said Julie, stepping into the large foyer, "And I brought you a gift." Julie held up the bag for Margo. A smile spread across her face and she excitedly clapped her hands together.

"It's not that exciting I'm afraid," Julie said, trying to temper the girl's expectations.

"What do you say, Margo?" her mother asked.

"Thank you," said Margo, taking the bag. "I know what to say. I'm not a little kid, you know."

"Nine going on sixteen," Lindsay said to Julie.

"And this is for you," said Julie, holding up the bottle of wine.

"Oh, you shouldn't have. That's so nice of you. Will you have a glass with me?"

"Absolutely. It smells wonderful in here."

"Irish stew," said Lindsay. "I make it every Christmas instead of turkey."

"Hot chocolate!" exclaimed Margo, pulling the package from the bag. "Can I have some, Mommy? Please? Thank you, mommy's new friend."

"Yes," said Lindsay, "you can have some, and her name is Julie."

"You're most welcome, Margo," said Julie.

They watched as Margo pulled at the tissue paper and unwrapped the gift.

"What is it?" Margo asked, holding it aloft.

"It's a dream-catcher," said Julie. "The Ojibwe people believe that if you hang it over your bed it will catch all your nightmares."

"Really?"

"Really."

"Mom, can I go hang it over my bed right now?" asked Margo.

"Sure, sweetie," said Lindsay. Margo took off running down the hall but then stopped abruptly, turning around. "Thank you, mom's new friend."

"It's Julie," said Lindsay. "Her name is Julie."

"Thank you, Julie," Margo shouted as she continued running down the hall.

"Follow me to the kitchen," said Lindsay. "That was sweet of you, and really, I can't think of a more perfect gift. She's been having these night terrors recently, or at least that's what I call them. I even took her to the pediatrician. She told me she was too old for night terrors, but Margo wakes up in the middle of the night screaming, her eyes wide, clawing at the air as if she's being attacked. The only way I can calm her down is bringing her into my own bed, and that can prove to be rather challenging at the best of times. So I hope your gift, even if it's only a kind of psychosomatic soother, will help her in some way."

"Does she remember anything when she wakes up?"

"Not much. She says she's had a nightmare, but can't say what it was about. All she knows is that she's had some sort of terrifying experience. I wish I could help her but I can't. Maybe your gift will bring her some peace."

"I hope so," said Julie, stopping near the kitchen island.

"Such cheery Christmas conversation. Here, you open that while I deal with my stew," said Lindsay, passing her a corkscrew. "The glasses are behind you, in that cabinet."

"Shall we make some hot chocolate for Margo?"

"Good idea. I'll throw on the kettle."

"I've been having bad dreams too, for a long time," said Julie at length.

"Because of what happened to your daughter?" asked Lindsay. She paused and shook her head. "Sorry, I didn't mean to get so personal. I think my filter is broken sometimes."

"No, that's okay. You didn't say anything wrong. And to answer your question, they began years before that," said Julie, popping the cork.

"Mom, I need help with this. Can you get me a nail or something?" Margo shouted.

"Okay, just give me a sec," Lindsay shouted back. "Can you stir this and watch the kettle? I'll be right back."

Julie took advantage of the opportunity and worked quickly. From her left pocket she pulled a finger of crushed pills and dumped them into a Mickey Mouse mug she found in the cupboard. She tore open the hot chocolate package and dumped two big scoops over the medication. "Hurry up and boil you son of a bitch," she whispered to the kettle. She snagged two wine glasses from the cupboard and shook a finger of pills from her right pocket into one, followed by some wine. A few grains of pill bobbed to the surface and gravitated to the edge of the glass. "Shit," Julie muttered. She opened several drawers in search of cutlery. Finally she found a spoon and quickly scooped off the residue.

"What are you doing?" asked Lindsay, stepping into the kitchen.

"Piece of cork floating in there, just trying to get it out," Julie said. Lindsay took the glass from her and held it up to the light.

"Looks good enough to me," she said, taking a sip.

"How is it?" asked Julie.

"Mmmm, that's lovely. Cheers," said Lindsay, raising her glass. Julie raised hers and took a small sip. The kettle made a snapping sound indicating it was ready. Julie moved toward it but Lindsay intercepted her.

"You're the guest. Relax," she said.

"Can I stir it?" asked Margo, strolling into the kitchen. She grabbed a spoon from the counter and waited for her mother to pour. Julie envisioned pieces of pill floating to the top, and Margo asking what these strange bits were. Maybe she could say they were bits of marshmallow? All she could do was watch as Lindsay tipped the kettle and steam rose from the mug.

Margo stirred.

"Stir it well or you'll get clumps," Lindsay said. "I'll get you some milk."

"Marshmallows too?" asked Margo.

"Okay, marshmallows too."

Julie felt a bead of sweat roll down her neck. She realized she was holding her breath and exhaled slowly, watching as Lindsay carefully poured tiny marshmallows from a bag into her daughter's cup. "More, more," cried Margo.

"Do you want some hot chocolate with those marshmallows?" her mother asked.

Margo nodded.

"Fine, but only because it's a holiday and we have a guest."

Margo clenched her fists and bounced with excitement.

Lindsay took a sip of wine. "Would you and your husband care to join us for dinner?"

Before Julie could answer, Margo interjected, "Can I go watch Wizards of Waverly Place?"

"Yes," said Lindsay. "And be careful not to spill that."

Margo toddled off, carrying her mug with both hands.

"Sorry about that," said Lindsay, turning back to Julie. "As I was saying, would you and . . . sorry, I forgot your husband's name?"

"Ryan."

"Would you and Ryan care to join us for dinner? It's just the two of us tonight and we'd love the company."

"Oh, that's very nice of you, but we're going to his parents' for dinner."

"I assumed you had some sort of plans, it being Christmas and all." Lindsay sipped her wine. Julie noted she had drunk about a third of it.

"That's really nice of you to ask. When you're back, we'll have you guys over."

"I don't know what it is, but I'm so happy to have met you. You're like the sister I never had. Sorry, does that sound weird? I mean, we just met each other really."

"Doesn't sound weird at all. I feel like I've known you for years," said Julie, sipping her wine.

"So what were you saying about your bad dreams?"

"I've been having this recurring nightmare for the last four years about the same two people."

"Really?" said Lindsay as she backed her way to the stove to stir her stew. "Tell me more."

"Well, we're all on a train and it's going along fine, and then out of nowhere it crashes. There's fire, smoke and the horrible sounds of metal twisting and popping. The woman sitting across from me is screaming at me to help her husband who's bleeding badly. She's begging me to help her husband, and I can't get my seatbelt off. It's stuck," said Julie, making it up as she went along.

"Then what happens?"

"Then I usually wake up."

"The same two people, for four years?" Lindsay sipped her wine, draining it close to empty.

"Do you want to hear something really freaky?"

"For sure."

"Well last week I was in a store, a coffee shop, and I looked across the shop and there they were."

"No way! Oh my God, what did you do?"

"Well exactly, right? What would you do?"

"I don't know. I'm totally freaked out right now. Are you sure it was them, the people from your dream?"

"As sure as I know I'm standing here in your kitchen right now."

"Holy shit," said Lindsay, draining the last of her wine. "So what did you do?"

"I waited for them to leave and followed them. Turns out they lived only a block away from the coffee shop. They had out their recycle bin out and I grabbed a piece of junk mail with their name on it. J. Franklin."

"Boy, this wine is going straight to my head. I feel dizzy."

"Maybe you should sit down?"

"Think I will," said Lindsay, taking a seat. "So then what?"

"I called the train station and pretended to be Mrs. Franklin. I said my husband had booked us two tickets and I wanted to confirm the dates."

"What did they say?"

"They gave me the dates. They were booked on a train to Toronto next week."

"That's unbelievable. What did you do?" said Lindsay with a slight slur in her voice.

"Nothing," said Julie flatly.

"What do you mean, nothing? You can't let them get on that train. You have to warn them. Boy I feel lightheaded," Lindsay said.

Julie didn't say anything at first. Maybe she shouldn't have gone this route. Maybe drugging them was unnecessary. She looked at Lindsay. There was no way to know for sure.

"Here's the thing," said Julie. "I lied."

"What do you mean you lied? You mean you didn't meet them?"

"No, I met them alright, except that it wasn't a husband and wife. It was a mother and daughter, and it wasn't a train but a plane," explained Julie.

"I'm sorry, I'm not following you," a puzzled Lindsay slurred.

"You and your daughter. I've been dreaming about you and your daughter for four years. You can't get on that plane tomorrow or you will both die."

"That's not funny," said Lindsay, her tone turning serious.

"I'm not kidding about this."

"So when you saw us . . ."

"I saw you in the parking lot at South Keys. I couldn't believe you were real. I went and got a membership at the Y so I could meet you, to find out if you were planning on flying."

"I want you to leave please."

"Lindsay, please, let me . . ." Julie placed her hand on Lindsay's shoulder. She jerked away.

"Don't touch me. You're insane. You can't just dream people up. I want you to leave now."

Just then the phone mounted to the wall began to ring. Lindsay stood to answer it, keeping her eyes locked on Julie. Then she looked at the number on the phone. "Margo, honey, it's daddy on the phone!" she shouted. "Margo, come talk to your dad," she shouted again and answered the phone. "Hello," she slurred.

Julie didn't know what to do.

"No, I haven't been drinking," Lindsay said. "Just a glass of wine. . . . Wait a minute," she said, pulling the phone away from her mouth. "Did you put something in my wine?"

Just as she finished asking the question, Julie saw her eyes roll up in her head. Her eyelids fluttered and her knees buckled as the phone fell from her hand.

"Holy shit," Julie whispered as Lindsay collapsed to the floor. Thankfully she was still breathing. Julie stepped over her and picked up the phone. A man's voice grew louder as she put it to her ear.

"Lindsay! Can you hear me? Are you okay?"

Julie hit the end button and it went silent. The only sounds she heard were the bubbling of the stew and the TV laugh track from down the hall. She turned off the stove as the phone rang again. The area code was 669. Shit, thought Julie, when her husband is unable to reach her he'll call the police. She figured she had maybe twenty minutes before they broke down the door. The phone rang again and Julie ripped out the battery. She stepped over Lindsay and walked down the hall to find Margo asleep on the couch, her right arm dangling off the edge. Finding the remote, she turned off the TV. The ring of a cellphone chimed from somewhere down the hall, and she followed it to the front door. It was coming from Lindsay's coat pocket. She took it out and turned off the ringer, then reached back in and took out some keys.

14

The time it would take to tie Lindsay up wouldn't be worth the savings. The police would be here soon and Julie had to act quickly. She managed to get Margo dressed in her winter coat and hat without waking her, then went outside and started the Pathfinder. She cranked the heat knob to full red and flicked on the rear window defroster. On the floor of the back seat she found the snow scraper and went about brushing off the windows. There was a man across the street shoveling his driveway. He stopped and stared at Julie. She glanced at him but didn't make eye contact. After she was done, she tossed the brush back in the car and went back inside for Margo. The neighbour watched her as she went.

Margo was heavy; unbelievably heavy for a nine-year-old. Julie carefully laid her on the floor, put a toque on her head, and dragged her by the ankles to the front door. She was nervous she had given the little girl too much medication—saved from a plane crash but killed with an overdose. Julie pulled Margo's boots onto her little feet and tied the laces tight.

Julie stood over Margo, a foot on other side of her hips. "Upsy daisy," she said, bending down to grab her under the arms and swing her limp body up over her shoulder. Out the front door she went. She locked gazes with the man across the street once again. "Fuck," she muttered.

Julie treaded carefully down the icy walkway. She could feel the man staring at her. She opened the back passenger door and slid Margo off her shoulder and into the backseat. Julie yanked her into a sitting position and fastened the seatbelt around her. Margo's head slumped down. Julie tried to push it up, but it sagged back down again. She left it alone. After making sure Margo's feet and hands were safely in the car, Julie stood up and shut the door. The neighbour was standing beside her.

"What's wrong with Margo?"

"Oh, you scared me," said Julie, startled.

"What's wrong with Margo?" repeated the man. "Who are you?"

"Margo has a high fever and I'm taking her to CHEO. I'm Lindsay's sister," Julie lied as she stepped around the man to the driver's door. The man followed her.

"Why isn't Lindsay taking her? Where's her mother?" he asked.

Julie ignored him. She opened the driver's door, hopped in, and slammed it shut behind her. She locked the door.

The man pounded on the window. "Where's Lindsay? She never mentioned having a sister. What's your name?" he shouted. Julie ignored him, shifted the stick to drive and hit the accelerator. The wheels squealed, spinning on the ice until they caught a piece of asphalt and shot the vehicle forward. It was more aggressive than Julie had wanted, but at the same time, if she was really going to the hospital, then this was how she would be driving.

"CHEO is the other way," yelled the man as Julie turned out onto the street. "Shit," she said, watching in the rearview as the man waved his arms repeatedly. Julie reminded herself why she was doing this. Lindsay—a Lindsay from a future that may or may not exist—had asked Julie for four years, begged her for four years, to save the little girl now slumped in the backseat. Save her. I will, thought Julie. I will.

She drove down Alta Vista Drive until it spit out onto Bank Street. From there she went south, past the shopping centre where she'd allegedly tried to commit suicide, the same place where she had run into Lindsay and Margo. It was the banality of the place which struck her: a grocery store parking lot of a strip mall on the edge of suburbia. Why there of all places? Bizarre, she thought, and then her mind refocused: Where to go? What if Margo wakes up? She would have to re-drug her.

Ahead on the left she saw the beige, six-storey façade of the Southway Hotel. She signalled and pulled into the parking lot. She figured she'd get a room, wait out the night, and leave Margo to be found in the morning. She would have missed her flight by then. Was it a sound plan? Not really, Julie thought, but it was the only plan she had left. As she turned off the engine she thought about calling Zola. That would be pulling her in, making her an accomplice. Lil had already been deemed crazy, but she wouldn't do that to Zola. Julie twisted in her seat and looked at the sleeping Margo. "How am I going to get you inside?" she asked aloud. She would think of something, but first things first. She pulled on the door handle and stepped out into the cold night wind, trudging her way across the parking lot into the warmth of the hotel lobby. She stood in line behind a couple and their two teenaged children. A man in a suit stood ahead of them at the counter. Eventually the clerk passed him a key, and he walked away pulling his suitcase behind him. The family advanced. Another clerk appeared and waved Julie over.

"How can I help you?" she asked. Her silver nametag read Britney.

"I'd like a room."

"Do you have a reservation?"

"No."

The clerk sucked air in through her smiling teeth. "I'm afraid we're completely booked up."

"Can you double check?"

"I'll check for you." The clerk tapped a keyboard a few times before finally reporting, "Yeah, I'm sorry, we have nothing. This is our busiest time of the year."

"That's okay. Thanks anyway."

"So sorry."

Julie crossed the lobby and exited the hotel through the automatic doors. She'd go to a motel, somewhere she could access the room directly from outside. It would be easier to smuggle Margo in. Maybe it was a blessing the hotel didn't have a room. It would have been difficult to get Margo past the front desk.

Halfway back across the parking lot, Julie sensed it. There was something wrong. Then she heard it, the short double chirp of police sirens. Two police cruisers turned into the parking lot. Julie spun around and saw another car enter from the other end. No way out. Maybe she could drive over the embankment and down over the sidewalk onto the road. She would be caught. A cruiser door opened and a police officer got out.

"Julie Cooper?" said the cop.

"Yes," answered Julie.

"Where's Margo?"

Julie knew they would find Margo; the car was only fifteen metres to her left. There was no point in stalling. But she needed to make sure they didn't get on that plane. She reached into her pocket and grabbed her cellphone. Zola could verify it. Or least make a case to Lindsay about why they shouldn't fly.

"Put it down," yelled the cop.

Julie ignored the officer. She turned the phone on and hit the contact button.

"Drop it!" screamed the cop.

Julie scrolled to the bottom of the contacts and hit Zola's number. She turned toward the police bringing the phone to her ear.

It was simultaneous, the sound of the gun and the impact of its bullet, and the force of both spun Julie around. Somehow she kept her balance and ended up coming full circle. Then she heard the gun again and this time she fell hard to the ground. She couldn't breathe. She tried sitting up.

"It's a phone," somebody was yelling. "We need a bus!"

Julie tasted blood. Somebody was standing over her telling her it was going to be okay, telling her to hang on, that an ambulance was on its way.

"Save her," Julie managed to say. She was cold. People were pressing on her, on her chest. She screamed. Time telescoped. Somebody with a stethoscope placed an oxygen mask over her face. She heard "On my count, one, two, three," and felt herself lifted into the air. She was placed into an ambulance. She saw the Pathfinder with Margo slumped inside.

Julie closed her eyes and found herself thinking about the Olympics, about how she had watched her friend on TV come in second last in her heat. But then at least she'd gotten to go. I almost made it, she thought, and then she fell unconscious.

15

An antiseptic smell greeted her as she awoke. And severe pain in her jaw. She swallowed and opened her eyes. White ceiling. White walls. A machine beeped to the pulse of a heartbeat. She tried to move but there was pain in her chest—hot, sharp pain. Looking down her arm, she saw a tube sticking out of it. She turned her head and followed it to an IV bag, beyond which sat a policeman staring at the TV mounted to the wall. His eyes were wide, his face grim. It wasn't the expression a cop should be wearing sitting in a hospital watching over a patient like Julie. His face was far too serious for such dull work as watching over an unconscious patient. She turned her head to see what it was he was so engrossed in.

"What you see here is an aerial shot of the wreckage where the plane crashed in the parking lot of this Ottawa shopping centre."

Julie's eyes widened. On the TV appeared the black smouldering wreckage of a jet strewn across a parking lot.

"For those of you just joining us, we are looking at the devastating crash of Air Canada's Flight 479 bound for San Francisco. There is no confirmation yet, but there appears to be no survivors of the hundred and ten passengers and crew who were onboard the Airbus 320. Witnesses reported seeing some sort of explosion shortly after takeoff. Dozens of people have reported seeing the plane on fire, smoke billowing from its fuselage, as it crashed into the parking lot we're seeing here. It appears the pilot may have tried unsuccessfully to land the plane."

"No," said Julie. "No, no, no." As she sat up, she realized her other arm was handcuffed to the bed rail.

"Take it easy," said the policeman. "I'll call the nurse." He got up and stepped out of the room. Julie stared at the TV. A man was describing what he saw, using his hand to demonstrate how the plane rotated in the air.

Julie's eyes filled with tears. She hadn't stopped it. Everything she'd tried had been in vain. She couldn't breathe. Her chest throbbed. The room spun. The beeping of the machine accelerated quickly, its rapid oscillation climbing to a high-pitched screech.

The door of Julie's room burst open and a team of doctors flew inside.

"She's crashing! Get me the cart!"

The little boy walked along a path in the shiniest of shoes. They looked old-fashioned, almost like they might belong on a doll. With his navy pea coat and straight, blonde, pageboy haircut, the child appeared to be from a different era. Around his wrist a piece of string, travelling upwards to a big red balloon bobbing above his head. He was walking with his parents and a small dog on a leash. The boy and the dog played as they all ambled along, the balloon causing the dog much distress. Again and again it leapt into the air, trying to bite the balloon. The child laughed. His parents laughed too. The boy lowered his arm, and the dog jumped and snarled, eventually catching hold of the string. It twisted and shook its head until the balloon came loose. Up it flew, away from the boy. His father tried to grab for it, but it was too late. The dog spat a tirade of barks at the ascending balloon as the boy began to cry inconsolably. Up, up went the balloon, until it was little more than a speck in the pale blue sky.

A bright flash. A flickering light. Everything slowly returning to focus.

"Julie, can you hear me?" somebody asked.

"Pulse is low but steady," somebody else said. "She's back with us."

Epilogue: 10 months later

Her stride lengthened, and her breathing synchronized with her steps. The running high was kicking in. Julie felt good. Reaching down, she grabbed her water bottle from the bottom of the stroller and checked her watch: 5KM, 32 minutes. Not bad, she thought to herself, considering I have to push this along. At Dow's Lake she turned to head back home. A cold hard gust of wind blew down a yellow rain of maple leaves, swirling and twisting around her. She stopped, unzipped the plastic cover of the stroller, and looked in at her sleeping son.

"Julie!" shouted a woman running toward her.

"Hi, Lindsay."

"I thought it was you," Lindsay huffed, coming to a stop. "Boy you're fast. Didn't you just have a baby for Christ's sake?"

Julie laughed. "That was over a month ago."

"Exactly. Anyway, the turkey's in the oven. I made the pumpkin pies last night. Margo's so excited to show you because she helped."

"We can't wait. Are you sure we can't bring anything over?"

"Positive. Let me look at Mr. Handsome."

Julie peeled back the stroller cover.

"Oh my God, he is gorgeous."

"He looks exactly like his father."

"Well don't tell him I said that or it'll go to his head," Lindsay laughed.

Julie re-zipped the stroller cover and asked, "Are you running back with me?"

"If I can keep up with you."

"I'm sure you'll be fine."

Somewhere a dog barked. Julie looked across the park and saw a boy with a red balloon.

"Wait, hold up," she said, grabbing Lindsay's arm.

"What's up?"

"Just wait here, I'll be right back."

Julie took off running across the park. Ahead of her, the boy and the dog were playing with the balloon. The boy lowered his arm, and the dog jumped and snarled, eventually catching hold of the string. It twisted and shook its head until the balloon came loose. Up it flew, away from the boy.

Julie snatched the balloon from the air.

"Saved it," she said, smiling. The dog was beside itself.

"Oh thank you," said the boy's mother.

"Dumb luck," said Julie, passing the balloon to the father.

"What do you say, Andrew?" he asked his son.

"Thank you," said Andrew meekly.

"You're welcome."

Julie smiled and jogged back to Lindsay.

"Did you know that was going to happen?"

"Did I know what was going to happen?"

"That the kid was going to lose his balloon."

Julie grinned. "A kid puts a tall glass of grape juice on the edge of a counter wearing a brand new shirt. What could possibly go wrong?"

"Are they going to die in a plane crash?"

"Not that I know of."

"Hmm, interesting. How will the turkey turn out?"

"Fabulous."

"Have you had any other dreams, like the kind you had about me?"

Julie smiled and shook her head.

"What?"

"Nothing."

"What is it?" Lindsay asked.

"Well, it's the first time you've asked me that."

"I . . . I didn't really want to know. I mean, what if you dream that I'm in a car crash or something. Then every time I get in a car I'll be paranoid."

"Rest assured, I haven't been dreaming about you *or* Margo."

"You would tell me if you did, though, right?"

"Absolutely. Now come on, let's run."

Julie hadn't lied, not technically anyway. She hadn't dreamt about Lindsay or Margo. But she wasn't ready to tell her friend about the new dream, the one waking her in the middle of the night and leaving her sheets soaked in sweat. Julie hadn't told Ryan about the new dream either. She was hoping it would stop, hoping it would go away. But so far it hadn't.

Julie was dreaming about a different woman about to die. She was dreaming about herself.

ACKNOWLEDGEMENTS

I want to thank the City of Ottawa for the grant that allowed this book to be created. Thanks for continuing to support the arts in this great city of ours.

Nicole Hillmer, Jeffrey Hodgson, Michael Dennis, Ross Buskard, and my mother Judith Gustafsson, thanks for reading, as always.

A very special thank you to real life athlete Ann Coros-DeCou for your great suggestions, especially on all things related to running and exercise.

Lisa Gregoire, my great appreciation for pulling out your red pen and giving it the once over.

To my publisher, Chris Needham, thanks for believing in this book. Word.

Marty Carr, my second sets of eyes, love of my life, there are no words.

Henry and Molly, my kids—love you like mad. Read this one when you're older.